KU-372-342

CHAPTER 1

"Just chill."

That is what Isaiah is telling me to do. But I'm finding it hard because he's icing a mountain of cupcakes in the kitchen and the school bell will ring in fifteen minutes. It would be a lot easier to chill if I could walk to school by myself.

"Why couldn't you have just bought Asda cakes like a normal person?" I sigh, sitting down at the table. I hope sitting here with my school bag across my shoulder will make him ice quicker but it doesn't, of course. As usual, Isaiah goes at his own pace.

"Being normal never gets you anywhere," he says, delicately adding golden stars to each cupcake. I watch in frustration, realizing that he has at least ten cupcakes lined up on the counter that haven't been touched yet.

I look at the time. We're going to be late, which means that I'll have to walk into my form room as Mr Adams reads out the morning notices. I'm not bothered about missing the notices though, they're always the same. Mr Adams, my form tutor, gives us a boring lecture about how the overuse of our mobile phones and the smartness of our school uniform will determine the rest of our lives.

What I'm worried about is that Mr Adams will stop mid-sentence for me to explain why I'm late, and this means that everyone will be listening. It's alright for Isaiah. He doesn't feel his cheeks burn and his palms go clammy when walking into a group of people, like I do, so he doesn't understand why I panic when we're late in the mornings.

I clutch the straps of my school bag and take deep breaths. Miss Scott, the teaching assistant in my form group, said that I should count to ten whenever I feel anxious – which happens to be all of the time when I have Isaiah as a big brother.

Isaiah is *far* from normal. If he's not winning science competitions or protesting social injustice, he's baking cakes for the school charity bake sale or playing the drums in the school band. He is the poster boy for everything you can accomplish if you follow the school's motto: ASPIRE, ACHIEVE, SUCCEED.

"Relax, no one is going to be staring at you," he says as I complain for the millionth time. He puts a lopsided iced cupcake in front of me as a way to calm my nerves.

"I don't need a cupcake; I need you to hurry up," I say pushing the iced chocolate cupcake away. He carries on creating iced swirls as I put my head down in defeat.

I was worried about this when I first found out that I was going to Daisy Mill Academy. Miss Cassidy, my Year Six teacher, made everyone in my class write down their worries about moving up to secondary school.

My list included:

- Being away from my friends.
- Having to meet new people.
- <u>Isaiah.</u>

Miss Cassidy told me that I didn't have to worry. Most of my friends were starting at Daisy Mill too. Only Yasmin Bhatti and Louis Harrow went to a different secondary school. She said that I wouldn't just have my friends from primary, including my best friend Zarrish, but I would also make new friends. As for Isaiah, she told me how lucky I was to have a big brother like him to show me the ropes of secondary school.

Well, Miss Cassidy, it turns out you were wrong. Big time.

I'm the only person from my primary school in my new

form group. It's now March and I haven't made any friends since starting Year Seven last September. Meanwhile, Zarrish is in a different form group and hasn't found making friends hard at all. The only lesson that I actually like is PE, and that's just because the form groups are mixed and Zarrish and I are together. Besides PE, all of my other lessons are truly awful. During the first week of school, every single teacher had the exact same reaction when I answered my name on the lesson register.

"Who is Storm Williams?" my teachers asked scanning the classroom. Each time I raised my hand warily, knowing what was coming next.

"How wonderful it is to be teaching Isaiah's little sister," they beamed.

The sparkle in their eyes soon faded when they realized that I'm nothing like my big brother. Unlike Isaiah, I don't get the best grades and I definitely don't get involved in school activities. I'm not on the student council or the debate team, and I definitely don't play an instrument like Isaiah. I was worried about coming to secondary school and having so many teachers, but most of them have already given up on asking me to contribute to class discussions or share my work with everyone at the end of the lesson. Even when I've got the answer right, the awkwardness of me nervously stumbling over my words makes me feel like I've got it all wrong.

My absolute worst lesson is maths. My form tutor, Mr Adams, teaches my maths class and I spend all lesson trying to keep up with him, which isn't easy because he speeds through questions like he's entering a competition for the most equations spoken in a minute.

I liked English at first, when we were writing, but now we're reading aloud and Mrs Osei makes everyone have a turn. I can't even follow the story because I'm too worried about speaking aloud, and then it gets to my turn and I have no idea where we're up to. Then I get flustered as I try to find my place on the page. It's awful. It's not that I can't read. I can. I just hate everyone listening to me read. Even though my eyes are glued to the page, I can feel everyone staring at me and it makes my voice shake and my mouth dry. When I eventually finish reading, I spend the rest of the lesson thinking about how terrible I was.

Then there is Isaiah. Isaiah is everywhere, yet never where I need him to be. Like right now, I need him to be out of the door so we're not late. I need him to stop talking to people for twenty minutes after school, so I'm not waiting in the dining hall on my own. I need him to stop being such a show-off, so that everyone stops calling me "Isaiah's little sister".

I look at my phone again.

"Isaiah, we have ten minutes!"

I don't know why Mum insists that we have to walk to school together. It's only across Princess Road and through Alexandra Park. Besides, if something did happen – like a lightning strike or we get kidnapped by aliens – I don't know what Isaiah is going to do about it. He's tall and scrawny just like me. Maybe he could bore our kidnappers to death with his knowledge of computer code or his rants about how we're all going to kill the planet with our selfish consumption of plastic and fast fashion.

"Why are you two still here?" Mum says, coming into the kitchen through the back door. She has to sidestep into the doorway to avoid the buckets of cement that have taken over our garden. Mum is having her dream kitchen put in. She says that the new kitchen will be better than our current one because it will have an island, and that's all Mum has talked about for ages. Her dream is currently a nightmare though. There are pipes and concrete and sawdust everywhere. She keeps the back door open for Minnie, our over-energetic boxer dog, who is too busy eyeing up squirrels on the bird feeder to come inside. I point to Isaiah with a scowl.

"Isaiah Jackson Williams! Could you have not done that

last night?" Mum tuts, reaching for a cake tin big enough to fit Isaiah's cupcakes.

"I had to wait for the cakes to cool," Isaiah says, reaching for more sprinkles.

"Careful man," he shouts, taking the tin away from her. Mum gives him *the look* and he quickly goes back to icing.

"Can I not walk to school by myself?" I plead.

Mum shakes her head. "No. Your brother is ready now," she says, turning back to him. "Isaiah, come on now, be fair to your sister please."

Isaiah kisses his teeth. "I'm trying to save the planet here."

"With cupcakes?" I laugh, fixing my unruly black curls into a bun. It doesn't last very long, so I give up, allowing my curls to fall in whichever direction they choose.

"These cupcakes are going to help build a well in Zambia. I don't see you doing anything to help."

I put my bag on my shoulder and march out of the kitchen, shaking off the flour dust that has somehow managed to cover my school blazer. I dodge past Mum's roller skates and the musical instruments that Dad has lined up to take to his next gig to reach the front door.

"I'm ready," Isaiah declares, shoving past me without a single speck of flour or icing on his immaculate school uniform. Mum follows us out of the door and into the front garden.

"Straight home. It's family night tonight. We're going bowling like you asked for."

"We're going to have an after-school detention for being late!" I groan.

"Little sister, can you relax? How can they give me a detention? I'm Head Boy!" Isaiah smiles, opening the garden gate and heading across the road.

"I have a name, you know," I say, shaking off the last of the icing dust from my blazer before running after him, trying to catch up.

Sometimes I wonder how Isaiah managed to become Head Boy. He's always late and causes absolute chaos wherever he goes. I overtake him as he smiles at his phone that is constantly pinging. I get a stitch in my side as I pick up pace. As we reach the school gates, I see Mr Peterson, the Headteacher, closing the student entrance doors. I break into a run. Isaiah continues to stroll in his usual chilled-out fashion. Mr Peterson stands in the middle of the student entrance with his high-vis jacket on, shouting "Hoody off!" and "Pencil cases ready!" as he prepares to hand out detentions to the late arrivals. I think this is Mr Peterson's favourite time of day, except for after-school detention of course.

"Ah, Isaiah Williams, just the man," Mr Peterson grins as

we approach him. "I need you at lunchtime," he continues as people slip past him. I creep past too, grateful that my brother's popularity with teachers means that I've dodged Mr Peterson's inspection.

"Hide me!"

I turn round to see Ryan Taylor crouched down behind me.

"Don't look at me!" he whispers loudly, using my bag to sandwich himself between me and the wall to the Student Services office. He's pretty small so it covers him completely.

"Act normal."

My eyes move around frantically not knowing where to look. I see Ms Morrison walking past with her walkie-talkie in hand, her ultra-high heels limiting her speed. She's holding a football that has *Property of Ryan Taylor* scrawled across it in big letters. Ms Morrison is my science teacher, who also happens to be the Deputy Head. She's in charge of behaviour, so she's stricter than most teachers. I used to like her because she has curly hair like me. Except her hair is much shorter and dyed red, which is totally against school rules. I guess teachers have their own rules. Her brown skin is just a shade darker than mine and I'm not too sure if her oval-framed glasses are for her eyesight or style, but she pulls them off. I stopped liking her when she made my entire class stay behind after a total fool (Ryan) threw a water balloon out of the classroom window and splashed a group of Year-Nine girls, who rushed up to our lesson for a fight. I watch as she walks over to Mr Peterson. He shakes his head and they both walk away.

"She's gone," I whisper as people walk past us and stare at the partially hidden Ryan behind me.

"Phew, that was a close one," he says, standing back up.

I carry on walking, hoping to get as far away from Ryan Taylor as possible. Ryan has caused nothing but trouble since the day we both started in September. If he's not throwing water balloons out of classroom windows, he's being chased by Year Tens for kicking their football up on the roof, or being told off for selling sweets in the schoolyard. Wherever Ryan is, a teacher is never far behind, ready to escort him to whatever punishment awaits. Unfortunately for me, Ryan is in my form and our surnames mean that we sit next to each other in most lessons, so his trouble is never far away from me.

"I was just playing footie against the wall. It's not my fault the ball hit the staffroom window. It was an accident!" he protests.

"Why do you have to make everything so hard for yourself?" I mutter, continuing my hurried walk to class.

"Says you!"

I stare at him. I wonder what he means by that, but I don't ask. Instead, I look at my phone again. I have two minutes to make it to form.

Ryan follows me up the stairs and down the corridor to our form room. I'm trying my best to walk as fast as I can, but I get stuck behind a group of Year-Ten girls, who aren't in nearly as much of a hurry as me. I try to look for a way round them, but I'm stuck. They don't seem to be able to walk and talk at the same time, and the way they keep stopping every time they burst into laughter makes me groan in frustration. I look at my phone. One minute before the bell goes. As I look around for an escape route, my eyes follow Ryan, who reaches up and taps one of the girls on the shoulder. As they turn round, they leave just enough space for Ryan to squeeze through without them noticing him.

"Yeah?" the scary-looking Year Ten snarls at me. I look towards Ryan, hoping to signal that it wasn't me who tapped her, but he disappears down the corridor leaving me alone.

"Did you want something?" she huffs. I rest my hands on my legs to stop them from trembling nervously. I shake my head and she turns round, not before giving me a dirty look. I walk silently behind them before they head into their form room, to my relief. I carry on walking but the sound of squeals getting closer with every footstep I take makes me slow down. I've managed to catch up with Ryan.

"Isn't Ms Morrison after you for kicking a football? You probably shouldn't be walking around with another one," I say, keeping one eye on the ball that is being thrown across the corridor.

"This isn't a football though, is it? It's a basketball," he grins.

"I don't think Ms Morrison cares what kind of—"

"Heads!"

Just as I'm trying to explain to Ryan that he doesn't make sense and is just going to get into more trouble, he hurls the basketball at Abdul – except it misses and hits the maths-office door. There's a pause. Everyone starts to scramble out of the corridor and I have no choice but to run too, as teachers poke their heads out of the maths-office looking for culprits.

I slow down at the sight of Mr Adams opening our form-room door.

"Got away with it," Ryan brags, dodging another teacher to make it safely into our form room.

I make it to my seat just in time as Mr Adams sits down at his untidy desk. He scratches the top of his wafer-thin brown hair, as he scurries round flicking through sheets of paper and muttering to himself. He pauses for a minute, his green eyes squinting as if he's trying his best to remember something. I cross my fingers hoping that he doesn't.

"Right, it's quiz time," Mr Adams remembers. He starts rummaging through piles of paper, kept under scientific calculators and protractors, to find the weekly quiz folder. I slouch back in my chair, disappointed that he didn't forget. Ignoring the tower of compasses that he has just knocked off his desk, he sits back on his chair, adjusting his Manchester United football tie that he never seems to take off. Mr Adams is just as chaotic as his desk. The calendar on the wall next to him hasn't changed since October last year and he always forgets to do the register until he gets a phone call from the attendance officer. The only thing he remembers is the behaviour policy. Our form holds the Year Seven record for uniform points and late detentions.

A chorus of groans ripples through the room at the announcement of the weekly quiz. I look at the clock on the wall. Form time is only supposed to be twenty minutes, yet it feels like the longest part of the day.

"Sir, can we choose our own groups for once?" Asha asks from the seat opposite me.

Mr Adams pauses to think about it. My stomach lurches. *Please say no. Please say no. Please say no.*

"Fine, but any messing about and you're back to working on your tables."

I watch as everyone leaps out of their assigned seats to their friends, while I stay glued to my chair in a swirl of panic. What should I do? I skim the classroom quickly. My hair feels itchy as the sound of giggling and chatter grows louder. I don't fit in anywhere. I always stick with Zarrish at social times and I don't speak up in class, so I've never spoken to anyone enough to be friends with them. I prefer it when the teacher has a seating plan, so I don't have to worry about who I sit next to.

"Storm," Mr Adams points to me, interrupting my panic. "Come on, hurry up and sit with a friend."

I put my hands on my face so nobody will notice that I've gone bright red. I look at Mr Adams hoping he'll just let me stay here on my own, but he's not noticing my panic. I'm not brave enough to tell him so my feet stay frozen as he looks at me with confusion.

"Just sit with Grace's table. Come on, we haven't got much time," Mr Adams says forcing me to move to the middle table. I stand up and glance over to Grace and the rest of her table, who give each other funny looks as I make my way over. Everyone on this table went to the same primary school. I think this is totally unfair, since I wasn't put in a form with anyone from my old primary school. As they've known each other the longest, they've always stuck together and never let anyone into their group voluntarily. I pretend I don't notice their disapproval of me joining their group and sit down, pulling my chair slightly away from them.

"Okay, first question," Mr Adams says. "What is the capital of Australia?"

I know this one. It's Canberra. I did a project about Australia when I was in Year Six.

"It's Sydney," Grace says, writing her answer down. She's wrong. I look round the table hoping someone else will correct her. Sara and Iman are sat texting on their phones. Lucy is asleep with her head on the desk and Jenna is talking to the group behind her.

"Come on, don't forget the winners will win a prize," Mr Adams mutters trying his best to sound enthusiastic.

"Name the national dish of France," Mr Adams continues. I know this one too, it's *Pot-au-Feu*. I learned that in French last week.

"Is anyone going to help?" Grace huffs, slamming down her pen.

"It's only a quiz," Iman shrugs, continuing to scroll through her phone instead of taking part.

"Yeah and the prize is only a box of chocolates," Lucy

yawns, using her school jumper as a pillow.

I look round the table as Grace grows impatient with her friends. I open my mouth to tell Grace the answer but she gets there before me. "Do you ever speak?" she asks looking at me, her eyes wide, as if she's expecting an answer. I do want to answer her. I want to ask her why she is singling me out when no one else on the table is helping with the quiz, but I can only manage a jittery shrug. Grace rolls her eyes as Mr Adams reads out the last few questions. I stay silent and flick through my planner so it doesn't make it obvious that I'm not joining in. I'm saved by the bell that rings out for period one. Once Mr Adams dismisses us, I rush out of the classroom, relieved that the form-time quiz is over for another week.

The doors to the PE department swing open, knocking me over as a group of Year-Eleven boys rush past. I manage to style it out by turning my tumble into a quick jump down the steps and see Zarrish waiting by our usual meeting place near the PE noticeboard.

"Hey!" I shout over to her, dropping my bag from my now throbbing shoulder and smiling as she walks over. Miss Scott is always telling me to put my PE kit in my locker, but it's on the top floor of F-block. Not only is that on the other side of school, but it's also in the sixth-form building. The one time that I did try to go to my locker, a bunch of sixth formers were blocking it. I walked past them five times but I was too scared to interrupt their conversation and ask them to move. I haven't been back since.

"Storm – finally!" Zarrish smiles waving a purple Pankhurst House slip in her hand.

There are four houses at Daisy Mill Academy: Turing House, Lowry House, Gaskell House and Pankhurst House. There are two form groups from each year group in each house. Luckily, my best friend Zarrish is in Pankhurst House like me.

"I've been called to Mrs Osei," she beams. My English teacher, Mrs Osei, is also head of Pankhurst House and being sent to her is not like being sent to Mr Peterson or Ms Morrison. As well as being called to her for giving cheek in lessons or fighting in the schoolyard, you can be called to Mrs Osei for good reasons too. Zarrish is never bad so she must have been chosen to do a house duty like giving visitors a tour of the school.

"Wait, does that mean you won't be in PE?" I ask, feeling my heartbeat quicken. My hands already feel clammy at the thought.

"I don't know, sorry," Zarrish says seeing the panic scrawled across my face. She holds out her purple slip to me as she takes out a polka-dot scrunchie to redo her high ponytail. I glance down at it. Mrs Osei's perfect handwriting makes it look more like a fancy wedding invitation than a note to go to the house office. It doesn't say when Zarrish will be back in lesson.

"I could only be a few minutes, although I hope it's longer so I don't have to get changed for PE," she says with a glint in her eye. "I'll meet you at our usual place at break if I'm not back in time.

"Don't worry, you'll be fine," she adds, although I'm not sure if she believes this herself.

I head towards the girls' changing rooms as Zarrish leaves through the PE doors. I've never done PE without Zarrish. I really hope that we don't have partners in today's lesson. I see Asha and Koko's things on the hook beside the front bench. They must have gone with Miss Scott, the teaching assistant for my class. The corridors become super crammed in between lessons; Asha leaves form early so her wheelchair doesn't get knocked. Koko only leaves early for PE and at lunchtimes, because she needs to go to the medical room to check her sugar levels. She has diabetes, so when she's high she drinks water and when she's low she has a can of Coke or a biscuit. Since Koko and Asha are the only girls from my form group in my PE class and Zarrish isn't here, I get changed as fast as I can. I pull on my PE top and place my uniform on the hooks quickly. I get more flustered as I root through my PE bag. I was so busy trying to get Isaiah out of the door this morning that I totally forgot that I'd left my trainers drying by the front doorstep. I have no choice but to go out onto the field in my black school shoes.

"Koko, stop doing cartwheels and sit down please," I hear Mr Harris, my PE teacher, bellow from the far end of the field. I walk past the football pitches and Astroturf to make my way to Mr Harris, who is over by the sandpit. I step on the white lines that have been painted on the grass to form track lines, looking for clues about what our new unit is going to be. "Come on, hurry up and sit down near the benches," Mr Harris shouts at the rest of my class, who are dawdling over. Mr Harris is wearing the same Oldham Athletic Football Club jacket that he wears every day. I like Mr Harris, because even though he spends way too much time gleefully reminding us that Oldham Athletic made it to the fourth round of the FA cup, he never raises his voice and he pretends not to notice when everyone uses the vending machine in the gym – which is supposed to be strictly for sixth formers only. I sit down cautiously on the wet grass, my hands on my shoes hoping no one will notice. Not caring how wet the grass is, Koko crashes down beside me. She takes a pen from her jumper pocket and begins doodling flowers on her hand.

"Today we will be starting athletics," Mr Harris announces. "Can anyone share any athletics events with the rest of the class?" Mr Harris asks.

I've seen athletics on the TV. I know that there is a one-hundred-metre and a two-hundred-metre race. I know about hurdles and relay races. There is also javelin and long jump.

"Nobody?" Mr Harris asks scratching his mousy brown hair.

Asha, who is just behind Mr Harris near the benches, raises her hand. Her hand dances in the air as Mr Harris scans the crowd for other raised hands.

"Like running, sir?" she blurts out, not waiting for Mr Harris's permission to speak.

"Yes, well done, Asha!"

Asha flicks her long shiny black hair behind her shoulders and sits up straight.

"I want everyone to line up on the beginning of the track," Mr Harris instructs, gesturing for the class to move with him across the field.

I stand back up and brush my hands dry, ducking out of

Koko's path as she keeps her eyes firmly on her doodling.

"Today we will be focusing on the four hundred metres, where you will run once around the track," Mr Harris says from the sidelines. Asha is beside him with her stopwatch in hand. The track is almost the entire length of the field and Mr Harris wants us to run all the way round? I've never run that far before. I stand on the starting line, my school shoes touching the freshly painted white lines on the grass. "Come on, Year Seven, this is a race!" Mr Harris claps his hands. Everyone barges to the starting line as soon as they hear that it's a competition. I'm elbowed a few times before I find myself at the back. So far in PE, we've only done badminton and orienteering. This is the first time we've had to go up against each other. As I look around at everyone else, my heart quickens and I wipe my clammy hands on my leggings.

"Is everyone ready?" Mr Harris asks, holding his whistle. I take a deep breath and try to shake off this morning. I try to forget about almost getting a detention for being late, because of Isaiah and his golden-sprinkled cupcakes. About Ryan Taylor and the scary Year Tens in the corridor. About Grace singling me out in the quiz, even though no one else was saying anything, and that Zarrish isn't here beside me.

"On your marks. Get set. Go!"

My feet spring off the starting line at the sound of the

whistle. I almost tumble to the ground, but I lift my arms outwards quickly to steady myself. I manage to regain my balance and I find myself zooming down the track. I close my eyes and feel the wind whooshing behind me.

"Who is that?"

I open my eyes immediately. I forgot where I was for a moment but as I look around, I see that I'm in the lead. I don't like the feeling of being out on my own with everyone watching, so I slow down gently to allow people to overtake me.

"Come on, Storm, keep going!" Mr Harris shouts. Some of my class turn round to see who Mr Harris is talking to before creating a clear path in the middle. I have no choice but to run between them, keeping my head down as I go. As I turn the bend of the corner, Teija Pritchard, from Zarrish's form group, zooms past me. Unlike me, she doesn't seem to care about the people around her – she shouts, "MOVE!" at the people who have decided to walk round the track.

She's captain of every Year-Seven sports team, so it doesn't surprise me that she sprints down the track at full speed. "Come on, Storm," Miss Scott shouts from the sidelines. "Ignore everyone else, just go for it," she calls, with an encouraging smile.

I think about it. Maybe I should follow her advice.

Just go for it.

I allow my feet to take over and sprint, fighting the urge to look back. I only look forward.

CHAPTER 2

"Storm Williams!" Mr Harris shouts, jogging over to me. "That was quality!"

No longer caring how wet the grass is, I sit down trying to catch my breath. I finished in first place. First place. I've never been first in anything.

"Hey, you're rapid! You flew straight past me," Teija Pritchard says flopping down beside me. I try to smile as I struggle to breathe through my exhaustion and excitement. This is also the first time that Teija, the most popular girl in Year Seven, has ever spoken to me.

Teija's friend, Jasmine, crosses the finish line and sits down next to her. "Did you win?" Jasmine asks. Teija sits up as more people cross the finish line and form a circle around us.

"No, I didn't. Storm did," Teija says.

"Who's Storm?" Jasmine asks. Everyone turns to look at me as Teija points in my direction.

"Oh, hi, Storm," Jasmine smiles.

I wish that I could say hi back but as I look round at the crowd of faces I'm now surrounded by, I can only manage to wave back awkwardly.

"Wait, who beat Teija?" Maya asks, sliding herself between Jasmine and Teija. Everyone shuffles round to make room for her.

"Storm," Jasmine says.

"Who's Storm?" Maya asks, looking around.

Everyone points in my direction again.

"I've never seen you before," Maya says, looking at me as if it's for the first time, even though we've been in the same PE class since September.

I feel everyone's eyes on me as they wait for me to say something but as my mind wavers for too long, the conversation swiftly changes and I've missed my chance to speak. I listen along to the chit-chat around me, watching the last remaining people cross the finish line and hoping Mr Harris will hurry up and announce the end of the lesson. Koko cuts across the track, but I keep this to myself as she crosses the finish line and sits down slightly further away from everyone. I wish I was sat at the back. Why did I have to sit here?

"Right, guys, it's time to announce the Pupil of the Lesson," Mr Harris finally says. I look towards Teija in anticipation; she usually wins Pupil of the Lesson in PE. "We have a girl who is not only the fastest in her class, but also has broken the Year Seven record for the four hundred metres. Give it up for Storm Williams!"

My eyes widen and a thrill of adrenaline dances around inside of me. I've never won Pupil of the Lesson before. My excitement fades as everyone's heads turn towards me. "Storm, you have to get up," Asha shouts over. I really don't want to get up in front of everyone, but I don't have a choice – Miss Scott, who is cheering loudly, reaches for my hand to pull me up. My legs feel like jelly as I walk over to Mr Harris, who is standing at the front with a huge grin on his face. Not every class has a teaching assistant; only classes like mine that need extra support. Sometimes people make fun of my class because we have Miss Scott helping us, but I'm glad she's with us, especially now. Her being beside me is the only reason I can stand here instead of wanting to run and hide.

Mr Harris rummages through his folder while everyone waits. I take deep breaths, trying my best not to look at the crowd. Every time the Pupil of the Lesson is announced in class I hope to myself that it won't be me, because it means that I will have to go to the front to get my postcard. But as I'm waiting for Mr Harris, a feeling of warmth starts to override my fear of standing up in front of everyone.

"Sorry, Storm, I must've left my reward postcards inside. Come to the office before the bell goes so I can find you one," Mr Harris says before dismissing us to the changing rooms. I look down at my school shoes, that are now completely covered in wet grass, and smile at the memory of crossing the finish line in first place. I want to do it all over again.

After I get changed, I wait by the PE steps that lead to the office for the bell to ring for break time. I hope that Zarrish is waiting for me at our usual meeting place by the windows in the dining hall. She won't believe that I was chosen to be Pupil of the Lesson. I can't believe it myself. I've never been picked for anything before.

"Storm, your brother is selling cupcakes at break, can you get me one?" Ryan says, suddenly appearing out of the boys' changing room and swinging his bag in circles above his head. I stand on the PE steps waiting for Mr Harris to find my postcard.

"Stop that please, Ryan," Mr Harris says coming out of the PE office with a half-eaten chocolate cupcake.

"Sorry, Storm, I don't seem to have any postcards left," Mr Harris says. "As soon as I get some, I'll bring one to you," he promises. I nod trying my best not to show that I'm disappointed that I'm leaving without my postcard.

"Hold on," Mr Harris says, squinting his face like he has just figured something out. "You're Isaiah's little sister?" he guesses, with a smile. I nod up at him. "How did I not realize this until now? It's obvious! You have the same freckles," he smiles. Both me and Isaiah have a sea of freckles covering our faces. It's usually what people notice first.

"He's just come round with his cupcakes. They're amazing," he adds taking a bite out of the icing. Isaiah spent all night and this morning making those cupcakes and Mr Harris demolishes one in seconds.

"Looks like you got all the sports talent though," he says. I can't help but beam a huge grin. I've never been told that I'm better than Isaiah at something before. "Never has anyone broken a record like that and you're not even wearing your trainers!" Mr Harris smiles pointing to my school shoes. "Don't worry, I'll let you off this time but make sure you bring your trainers next week," he says, noticing the panic now scrawled across my face.

"Yes, sir," I say quietly.

"I'm expecting you to smash every record when you have them on," he smiles. "You should come to athletics club every Tuesday after school and Thursday lunchtime," he adds, pointing to the extracurricular timetable on the wall.

I look at the photos of the athletics club on the wall and scan the past students gleefully posing with trophies. I really want to go, but it would definitely be too scary to go alone... maybe I can persuade Zarrish to go with me. After all, she was on the school football team in Year Six and—

"Ryan Taylor!"

Ms Morrison stops my thoughts in their tracks as she stands at the top of the PE steps. She's wearing her science lab coat with her customized sparkly goggles hanging loosely round her neck, as if she has just been interrupted from one of her science classes to step into Deputy Head duty to deal with Ryan. I notice Mr Harris hide his half-eaten chocolate cupcake behind his back as everyone else falls silent. Even the teachers get scared when Ms Morrison is around.

"Come with me," she demands.

I watch as Ryan sulks up the PE steps and follows Ms Morrison out through the doors. I guess he didn't get away with causing chaos this morning after all, but that's no surprise. He never does.

As soon as the bell goes for break, I follow the crowd to the dining hall to wait for Zarrish. I have to keep moving out of the way of people barging past. It's getting busy and I adjust my bag on my shoulder and look at the time. There is only five minutes of break left. I wonder where she could be.

"Storm!" I turn my head to see Zarrish finally walking in my direction.

"Sorry we took so long," she says. I go to open my mouth to tell her all about winning in PE and ask her if she will go to athletics club with me, but then I stop myself.

We?

A girl who I have never seen before stands next to Zarrish. "This is Melissa; she's new," Zarrish says. The new girl looks me up and down before smiling at me. Her fresh emerald-green Daisy Mill uniform gives me flashbacks to the first day of school, making me shudder.

"That's what Mrs Osei wanted me for. Melissa is in my form group and I've been made her buddy." Zarrish smiles proudly at her new responsibility. She continues to explain how Melissa spent two terms at St Margaret's but she didn't like it, so she moved to Daisy Mill. Zarrish has to show her round school and make sure that she settles in.

"How was PE?" Zarrish asks. All the tables are now full so we stay by the windows.

"It was good, yeah," I say quickly, adjusting my bag on my shoulder again. Maybe I should ask her about athletics club later when we're by ourselves.

"Isaiah's little sister!"

I turn round to see Talia and Princess, friends of Isaiah's, striding towards us. I'm amazed at Talia's complete disregard for the school uniform policy – she's wearing Nike Jordans, hoop earrings and a grey hoody – but I'm even more amazed that she got past the teachers who are on duty by the dining-hall entrance. Talia and Princess are in Year Eleven, like Isaiah. Talia gets good grades and takes part in extracurricular activities, so teachers let things like trainers and hoop earrings slide when she's the one breaking the rules. The same can't be said for Princess, who tags behind Talia with plasters covering her piercings and baggy trousers swapped for her usual black jeans.

"You're all in Pankhurst House, aren't you?" Talia says waving a clipboard in her hand. I nod hesitantly. "Well, we need to sign people up for Sports Day," Talia says, shoving the clipboard into my hand. I have no choice but to grab it before it slips through my fingers.

"Isn't Sports Day not for ages?" Zarrish asks, staring admiringly at Talia's neon-purple acrylic nails.

"Sports Day is next term and we are not losing this year, especially now that I'm House Captain," Talia declares proudly.

The House Championships are a huge deal at Daisy Mill and Isaiah told me that we lose to Turing House every single year. Besides general good behaviour and competitions, like the inter-house poetry slam and the bake-off during European languages week, the only other way to win the House Championships is on Sports Day. The House Championships winners are announced on that day. Mrs Osei has made it her mission to win the House Championships this year. With Talia as House Captain and Isaiah as Head Boy, we might finally stand a chance.

Maybe I should sign up for Sports Day. I mean, I did just break the four-hundred-metre record in PE. I almost take Talia's pen to sign up, but I wait to see if Zarrish does first.

"Can we think about it?" Zarrish decides.

Talia rolls her eyes at our lack of school spirit. "More people need to sign up if we're gonna beat Turing House in the House Championships. I'll come and find you again sometime," she threatens before heading into the Bistro.

"Bye, Isaiah's little sister!" Princess smiles, following behind Talia.

"You can't go in there, the Bistro is only for Year Tens and Elevens," Zarrish explains, watching Melissa follow Talia and Princess.

"That is so unfair." Melissa frowns holding onto the Bistro door to peer inside.

"Shall we show Melissa outside?" I suggest. I don't really

want to go outside but Melissa has one foot inside the Bistro and it's making me nervous.

Both Zarrish and Melissa must not have heard me as they continue to hover around the Bistro entrance.

"Who is that selling cakes?" Melissa asks, with a raised eyebrow. I creep closer to see who Melissa is talking about.

"That's Storm's brother," Zarrish says. Zarrish is the only person at Daisy Mill who refers to Isaiah as my brother, which makes a change from constantly being called his little sister.

"That's your brother?" Melissa says as if being Isaiah's sister is something impressive.

"Yeah, and he's so extra, isn't he, Storm? He's Head Boy," Zarrish says, trying to lead Melissa away from the entrance as Mr Peterson walks by.

"Well if he's your brother then you can go get us a cupcake," Melissa says turning to look at me.

"I can't go in. It's strictly only Year Tens and Elevens," I repeat. Melissa shrugs it off as if rules don't matter.

"You're not going to get into trouble. Just say you were showing the new girl round," she says, having it all figured out.

Feeling uneasy, I look at Zarrish for backup, but she's looking at me like she's unsure of what to do herself.

"Besides, they all seem to know you so they won't tell,"

Melissa adds pointing towards Talia and Princess, who now have a cupcake each.

I hesitate for a moment. I can't just waltz into the Bistro like it's a perfectly normal thing to do. Teachers are strict when it comes to the Bistro. Once Mr Peterson caught Ryan inside and even though the Year Tens tried to hide him under a table, Mr Peterson gave him a lunchtime detention.

Before I can say no, I feel hands on my back and my body lurches forward through the entrance. My heart skips a beat as I turn back round to see Melissa with the biggest grin on her face.

"See, that wasn't so bad, was it?" she smirks. Zarrish looks as shocked as I do that Melissa has just pushed me inside the Bistro, but she doesn't say anything. Instead, Zarrish's worry soon fades as she joins Melissa in the excitement of breaking a school rule.

The Bistro is a lot smaller than I imagined now I'm inside. It's packed but doesn't feel as chaotic as the dining hall. Each table is taken by groups of Year Tens and Elevens who are either chatting quietly, eating fancy pastries that aren't served in the dining hall or revising for exams. The stillness makes me feel uneasy. We could get caught at any second.

"What are you waiting for? Go get us all a cupcake before we get spotted," Melissa demands. The Bistro is half the size of the dining hall, yet Isaiah's cupcake stand feels like it's miles away. Melissa and Zarrish are both staring at me, so I have no choice but to walk over to Isaiah.

"Aren't you coming?" I whisper, noticing the two of them not following me.

"We don't want to make it obvious, do we?" Melissa points out.

"You need to hurry up," Zarrish says, eyes darting around.

Both Melissa and Zarrish gesture to me to hurry up, so I keep walking. Isaiah is going to get a shock when he sees me. I don't break the rules. Ever.

"Excuse me, you shouldn't be in here!"

I close my eyes, hoping it will somehow make me invisible. Whoever shouted at me is now standing in front of me. The smell of coffee and old books hits me instantly. It can only be one person: Mr Peterson, our Headteacher.

"You know the rules. Only Year Tens and Elevens," he says getting out his detention slip book from his tweed blazer pocket. I glance over to the entrance to see if Zarrish and Melissa are coming to rescue me. I hope they'll come up with an excuse to avoid a detention or share the punishment so I don't have to do it alone. But when I look over to the entrance, they're both gone.

I'm on my own.

I turn to Mr Peterson, who is searching his pockets for his pen. "Well come on then, let's hear your excuse," he tuts.

The photograph on his staff badge is faded but you can still make out his thick ginger hair, which is now grey and receding. Mr Peterson has been at this school long enough to have taught my dad and uncle. Isaiah says he isn't as scary as everyone makes out. He says you just have to get him on your side. I don't know how I'm supposed to do that. Not when he's staring at me, waiting for an excuse as to why I'm breaking one of his school rules. A lump catches in my throat and my eyes start to fill up with tears.

"Sorry, sir, I told her to come in to give me something," Isaiah says jogging over. He's holding a money box in his hand that jingles with the sound of coins.

"I'm run off my feet here raising money for the school charity. Please forgive me," Isaiah says. If Mr Peterson wasn't standing in front of me, I would have rolled my watery eyes at Isaiah for being such a show-off. Mr Peterson immediately closes his detention book. "I forgot we have another Williams at Daisy Mill," Mr Peterson smiles. "I'll let you off this time but make sure it doesn't happen again."

Isaiah shakes his head, "Yes, of course, sir."

Wow, Isaiah really is smooth. As we watch Mr Peterson walk away, Isaiah turns to me. "You spent all morning moaning about getting a detention and then you come into the Bistro?"

"I was pushed," I whisper.

"By who?" he asks, frowning.

His question makes me tense up. "It was a joke – chill," I say. Even though I don't find it funny that Melissa pushed me into the Bistro and then disappeared at the sight of trouble, I don't want Isaiah to make a scene about it. I leave the Bistro just as the bell goes. Zarrish and Melissa are nowhere to be seen so I start to head to my next lesson.

"Sorry we left you," Zarrish says, rushing in my direction down the corridor. She looks guilty, so I decide not to make a big deal about it.

"Where are the cupcakes?" Melissa says. I laugh awkwardly thinking she's joking but my laughter soon fades as she stares at me blankly. She's being serious.

"Didn't you see Mr Peterson almost giving me a detention?" I frown.

Melissa shrugs.

"Isaiah had to save me because I couldn't think of an excuse," I explain. They would have known this if they hadn't left me to face Mr Peterson on my own.

Melissa rolls her eyes. I stop talking, as she seems just as annoyed with me that I came back empty-handed as I am with her for almost causing me to get a detention.

"We have English now," Zarrish groans. I have English too, so I walk with them down the corridor and up the stairs to the English corridor.

"Excuse you," Melissa snaps as Koko barges past us impatiently.

"You're welcome," Koko shouts back. Melissa and Zarrish both pull a face at each other.

"That doesn't even make sense," Melissa says giving Koko a dirty look, which causes Zarrish to smile. I guess she's found someone who dislikes Koko too. Zarrish has never liked Koko, not since Koko was put in our group during Year Six transition day. Everyone's head turned when she strode to our table dressed in a rainbow-coloured pinafore which matched her multi-coloured hair extensions. Her outfit would have been shocking anyway but it was even more of a surprise, since we all had to wear our primary-school uniform on transition day.

"Who does she think she is? Put your bag on the chair so she doesn't sit next to us," Zarrish had said as Koko tried to find a seat at our table. Before she could sit down, she was quickly ushered into student services by Mr Peterson, who later returned Koko without so much colour. Little did I know then that I would be in a form group with Koko and not Zarrish.

"Wait, you're in her form?" Melissa smirks as I walk into my English classroom. "Wow, I feel sorry for you," she continues loud enough for everyone to hear.

"Who even are you?" Ryan says, sticking his head out of the classroom. Everyone inside the classroom laughs causing Melissa's cheeks to go red.

"She's new and her name is Melissa," Zarrish says.

"And don't forget it," Melissa scowls.

"Right, girls, lesson time," Mrs Osei says, stepping out of the English classroom and into the corridor.

Zarrish and Melissa both stop giving funny looks to my form group as they follow Mrs Osei's instructions and head to their lesson. I begin to make my way inside, but Mrs Osei blocks my path.

"Just wait here for a minute, Storm," she says, pointing to the edge of the corridor just before the stairs. I step back, dodging a few people dawdling.

Am I in trouble? When I first found out that I was in Pankhurst House and that Mrs Osei would be my Head of House, I wasn't surprised. You always get put in the same house as your siblings. I'm glad that I'm in Pankhurst, because everyone says that Mrs Osei is the best Head of House at Daisy Mill. Being Head of House means that she's in charge of pastoral care and I'm glad that I have Mrs Osei to watch out for me. Mrs Osei's personality matches her bright and colourful outfits. You can usually hear her coming by her boisterous laugh. It sends a ripple effect down the corridor as everyone else can't help but laugh along with her. Mum totally embarrassed me at Parents' Evening when she asked Mrs Osei for her skincare routine and said that she wished she could pull off her buzzcut.

I usually end up in Pankhurst House office when I get too upset and need a few minutes to calm down. Sometimes I get upset when I'm in new social situations, and when people fuss it causes me to get more upset, and before you know it I'm crying uncontrollably. It's so embarrassing. But when I'm in the office, Mrs Osei gives me plenty of encouragement, along with her warm smile, funny stories and emergency hot chocolate.

However, Mrs Osei can also be very scary. You don't want to be on the receiving end of one of her tellings-off. Respect is her middle name and if you cross the line, she will definitely let you know about it.

She must have heard about the Bistro. Maybe Mr Peterson told her about it and she thinks that I deserve a detention after all. As I wait for Mrs Osei to stop shouting at people who are in no rush to get to lesson, I can't shake off the bad feeling about Melissa. Maybe I shouldn't judge her so quickly. I always hate it when people judge me. Maybe she had a terrible time at St Margaret's, so she feels like she has to make a name for herself here. I think back to September when I first started at Daisy Mill. It was horrible. Getting lost every time I had to change classrooms, not knowing anyone in my new class and dealing with the older kids taking advantage of us being new by jumping the queue at lunchtime. Melissa has to go through all of that again.

"Hand the books out, I'll be in in a minute," Mrs Osei calls to the class, before stepping towards me. I cross my legs, to make it less obvious that they're shaking.

I try to remember Isaiah's excuse as to why I was in the Bistro. I wish I could be as smooth as he is. He gets away with everything. I open my mouth to give Mrs Osei my best excuse, but she speaks before I do.

"I've just got off the phone with your dad. There has been a family emergency," she says softly.

My mouth shuts immediately as my mind races. What kind of family emergency? Is it Mum? Dad? Grandma? Panic sweeps over me with worst-case scenarios. Is someone in hospital? Or is it Minnie? She's always running off in the park. What if she ran into the road?

"There has been a burst water pipe at home. Your dad is picking you up at the end of the day because you will have to go stay with your grandma, just until it's all sorted.

Your dad was very calm on the phone and said you mustn't worry."

That isn't very reassuring. Dad doesn't worry about anything. He could win an award for being the most chilled-out person on the planet.

"Right, I need some readers." Mrs Osei claps her hands as she leads me into the classroom.

I sit at my seat wondering what is left of the house and how long we'll have to stay at Grandma's. It must be something to do with the building work. The downstairs of our house already looked like a disaster zone; I can only imagine what it will look like now. It must be bad if we have to move out. What if everything is ruined? What if we can't go back?

"Ryan, I want you to be Macbeth," Mrs Osei says.

"Do I have to?" he moans, not lifting his head up from the table.

"Yes, and if you're good, I can write a nice report to Ms Morrison. She just emailed me for feedback about you," she adds, giving him the side eye. Mrs Osei hates it when people from Pankhurst House are in trouble.

Ryan tuts and rubs his eyes as he lifts his head up.

"Storm, please can you be Lady Macbeth?" she says. The butterflies in my stomach race around. Mrs Osei just told me that I have a family emergency because my house has flooded, and now she wants me to do the one thing I hate the most: read out loud! She can't be serious. A burst water pipe? What does that even mean? As I pick up the book to scan the pages for how many lines I have to say, I can only picture my house now submerged under water.

Ryan puts the yellow overlay that he uses to read across the pages that we're sharing and begins reading his lines. He gets more enthusiastic as the reading goes on, causing me to lose my place every time he uses the things around us as props.

"Storm, you need to speak louder, I can't hear you," Asha interrupts.

I rub my palms against my legs. I let Ryan hold the page open as I use my hands to help stop my legs from trembling.

I jump up at the sound of the door opening. "Can I borrow Storm for a minute?" Mr Harris says, walking in.

"Are you in trouble?" Ryan asks, swinging on his chair until Miss Scott stops him.

"How can Storm be in trouble? She never speaks," Abdul jokes and the class erupts into laughter as I jump up and walk out of the classroom, pretending not to hear.

"Here you are," Mr Harris says, handing me a Pupil of the Lesson postcard. "I told you I would bring it to you as soon as

I got hold of some. Hey, don't forget, I want to see you at athletics club," he smiles.

From the new girl to my house being flooded, this morning's PE lesson seems like a distant memory.

"Storm, it's your line," Asha says as soon as I go back into the classroom and sit down at my seat.

"We're on page forty-two," Mrs Osei reminds me as I take a deep breath, my mind still racing. I push my Pupil of the Lesson postcard to one side as I try to find my place on the page.

CHAPTER 3

I step inside Dad's car, soaked from the dreary Manchester rain and exhausted from trying to fight my way through the end-of-day school rush. Dad tells me how Minnie has already been banished to Grandma's garden for knocking over several of her vases and chasing next-door's cat down the street. I scan the boxes piled in the car labelled *Dad's Sound Equipment* and *School Uniforms*.

"How long are we staying at Grandma's house for?" I ask. Dad, who is tapping the steering wheel along to the music blasting from the car radio, fails to hear me.

"Dad?" I shout, tapping him on the shoulder and interrupting his rendition of *Hey Joe* by Jimi Hendrix. He jumps, slightly startled. He explains more about the house. A pipe in the kitchen burst and flooded the kitchen and the living room. The floors are ruined and everything downstairs, including all the furniture, needs replacing. But in true Dad fashion, he tells me not to worry.

"Go find your brother, he's been ages," Dad adds, quickly changing the topic of conversation. I tell Dad that there's no point trying to find Isaiah. He could be anywhere. He could be in the music department arranging the next school band performance, he could be in the Bistro arranging another social-justice campaign or he could be in Pankhurst House office, doing Head Boy duties. Zarrish was right earlier, he is always doing the most.

"There he is," Dad says, spotting Isaiah walking over and starting the car engine. As Isaiah tries to convince Dad to let him bring three bags of fabric and recycling material from the textiles department to Grandma's house, I notice Melissa walking out of the student services entrance with a tall blonde lady, who I assume is her mum. She notices me and waves cheerfully. Dad joins me in waving back until I give him a nudge. "What? I was just waving back. Is she a new friend?" he asks. I shrug. Do friends almost get you a detention or run away when you are getting in trouble?

"I can't leave them at school because I need to make Ms Morrison's dress by this Friday so I can start Mrs Osei's next week." My thoughts are interrupted by Isaiah and Dad's debate. I look away from Melissa, hoping that she isn't witnessing a classic Williams family drama.

"You're making Ms Morrison a dress?" I say as Dad gives in and Isaiah shoves his bags into the car. After the success of the bake sale this morning, Isaiah raised enough money to build a well in Zambia, so he has now turned his efforts into organizing an up-cycle fashion show to raise money for a school in Peru. It's like he's on a one-boy mission to save the world; I'm just not sure how he's going to save the world and complete his GCSEs at the same time.

"Ms Morrison is going to wear a dress made out of ring pulls, Mrs Osei is wearing a dress made out of an old tent and, well, we haven't decided what Mr Peterson is wearing yet, but he's agreed to do it so he can't back out now," Isaiah explains as we finally leave school half an hour after the bell rang.

I don't know how my brother managed to persuade the teachers to do this, but I'm going to make sure I have a front-row seat.

"It's going to be a tight squeeze at your grandma's house," Dad explains to Isaiah. "We have to respect your grandma's space."

"How much of a tight squeeze?" I ask, already struggling to move behind Isaiah's bags and wondering how we are all going to fit into Grandma's house when she lives in a two-bedroomed terrace.

"Well, your mum and I will be on the sofa bed in the living room and you two will be sharing the spare room," Dad says.

"Sharing?" Both Isaiah and I gasp at the same time in horror.

"It's only for a few nights, until the house is sorted. I'm sure you'll both survive," Dad says, tapping away on the steering wheel.

There is absolutely _no way_ that I'm going to survive sharing a room with Isaiah. There are too many reasons to explain why, but the main ones are:

Isaiah is super-chaotic, which doesn't go well with the fact he's always planning something. We're still finding snowflake shapes around the house after he organized the Year Eleven Christmas disco. (Zarrish still thinks it's unfair that the Year Elevens got a Christmas disco in the Bistro and we had to sing boring carols in the main hall.)

He is very messy. Once he pinched my felt tips, so I went into his room to get them back and I stepped in something slimy. When I looked down to see why my feet made a squelching sound, I saw that it was because I was standing in a greasy cold pizza that was left on the floor.

His room smells weird, probably because of the leftovers he keeps and the Lynx deodorant that he must bathe in because it's way too strong.

He plays his music LOUD. Not only is Isaiah in the school band, but he's also a DJ for school events and he's played a few birthdays too. Everyone says Isaiah got his musical talent from Dad, but now they like different music. Isaiah plays mostly drum and bass, and the *thump thump thump* of the beat always makes the walls shake, which Mum and Dad hate.

"Is family night cancelled tonight?" I ask.

"Sadly yes, but we can keep bowling for next week when we're back home and everything returns to normal," Dad promises. We have family night every Wednesday evening. It was Mum's idea a few years ago, after she was always working late shifts at the hospital and Dad was always on the road with his band. Wednesday evenings are now for family time only. We take it in turns to choose what we do and tonight was finally my turn again. I picked bowling, but it looks like we'll have to wait.

When we get to Grandma's house, I drop my school bag in the hallway and follow Dad into the kitchen. The smell of fried plantain and macaroni cheese hits me instantly. The only time we have a Sunday tea on a weekday is if something really bad has happened.

"Hello, Storm," Grandma smiles, walking into the kitchen with a sewing machine under her arm. She puts it on the table and brushes down her old jumper that is covered in paint splotches, which she seems to wear every time I see her. Grandma is an artist. She was even part of an exhibition where local artists were shown in Central Library. She gives me a hug and I feel more relaxed, until she releases me and I see that the paint from her jumper has transferred onto my school uniform.

"What a day this has turned out to be," Grandma laughs, sitting down at the table before uncovering a plate. Mum and Dad carry on stirring pots on the stove as Grandma reaches for a bite of fried plantain. She clearly doesn't mind that they've practically taken over her house.

"Isaiah requested my sewing machine as he raced up the stairs just now, but I can't carry it up so he'll have to come down for it," she says. "How was school for you?" she asks.

I suddenly remember today's PE lesson and I root through my pockets, taking out my bent postcard before sliding it across the table. "I got Pupil of the Lesson in PE for being the fastest girl in Year Seven. Mr Harris wants me to join the athletics club," I say with a smile. That's the first time I have told anyone about it all day. The combination of Mum's cooking and remembering today's PE lesson distracts me from the house situation.

"That's brilliant, Storm. You've always been good at

sports. I've always wished you'd take it further." Mum smiles, taking the postcard and showing it to Dad, who has just let Minnie inside.

I grimace at the memory of Mum and Dad trying to persuade me to go to netball after school at primary. Or the time they tried to get me to go to football on Friday nights at the community centre. Every time it would end with me having a meltdown before leaving in defeat. I felt too much pressure as people screamed at me to pass the ball and I dreaded when we had to pick our own teams. I always got left until last because everyone picked their friends first. As sporty as I am, I've never had the confidence to take part in anything, but today's PE lesson felt different. Running felt exhilarating yet calming at the same time. Crossing the line in first place was the best feeling in the world. I want to do it all over again.

"I might join athletics club but I have to ask Zarrish first," I decide. I'll text her now since I couldn't talk to her properly before.

Storm: Guess what? I have to share a room
with Isaiah.

Mum tells me to go up to my new room and see if they've

brought enough of my things.

"Isaiah!" I shout as I walk through the bedroom door. The bedroom used to be my dad's and uncle's when they were growing up. The posters on the wall are of movies and music from when they were teenagers. I could probably name all of them because Dad drags us all to Leeds Festival every year. I don't mind, because me and Mum stay in a hotel – she doesn't "do" camping, not even the fancy kind.

"Where am I supposed to go?" I ask, shoving Isaiah's clothes and guitar with my foot.

"Can you stop being dramatic?" he says before shouting, "Don't touch anything!" I roll my eyes and manage to dodge bin bags full of fabric to sit on the bed I guess is mine for the next few nights.

My phone pings.

Zarrish: Ew that is gross. I could never share a room with my brother.

Storm: Today's PE lesson was fun. I'm sad you missed it. I want to try athletics club at lunch tomorrow. Will you come?

I see her typing.

Zarrish: Isn't that like running?

Storm: Yes, but it's fun because we get to race.

I think about what might get her to do it.

Storm: I beat Teija in PE, I think she'll be there.

I can see that she is typing.

Zarrish: OK sure, let's go :)

I knew telling her about Teija would get her to come. Zarrish and Teija are in the same form, but they aren't friends yet, even though Zarrish always talks about her like they are. I can't wait for tomorrow now that Zarrish is coming to athletics club. I know that she's going to love it.

I put my phone down happily and decide to inspect the bags Dad packed for me. "Who's being dramatic now?" Isaiah says, watching me as I throw my school shirts and odd socks from the bags in a frenzy. I can't help it though. Dad's not brought my favourite hoody that I love to sleep in, or my bath bombs that I got from Lush for my birthday. He's also forgotten to bring my ocean light projector that helps me sleep at night. I really hope Dad has forgotten everything and I didn't leave anything downstairs at home. If I did, it will be in the rubbish tip now.

Most importantly, Dad has not brought my trainers that I know were safe because they were drying outside on the front doorstep. How am I supposed to go to athletics club now?

"Hey, guys," Isaiah says, waving to his friends, who are waving back on his laptop screen.

"Isaiah!" I shout, mortified as Talia and Jayden giggle at me, having just witnessed me turn my bags inside out. I duck under a pillow before I slide off the bed and crawl onto the floor, so that they can no longer see me as they start band practice or debate club or whatever they are up to next. I manage to make it out of the room before I hear my name being called from downstairs.

"Dad, you haven't brought my trainers," I say, rushing downstairs to ask him to go back and get them.

"Not now, Storm," he replies holding Minnie by the collar. A broken dish is on the floor with what looks like Mum's macaroni cheese.

"Take Minnie for a walk, eh?" Mum says. Grandma shakes her head and suggests a chippy tea to replace Mum's cooking,. I put Minnie, who looks unashamed and extremely proud of herself as she licks her lips, on her lead and head out of the door. As I reach Grandma's front gate, I freeze seeing the person sat on the pavement just outside.

You have got to be joking.

CHAPTER 4

"Howdy, neighbour."

Acting as if he's in a Wild West film, Ryan comes towards me as I step inside my period-four science lesson. With a wide grin across his face, he begins squirting people with pipettes, causing a squeal to echo round the classroom.

As if seeing Ryan at school wasn't bad enough, now I'm living next door to him. When Grandma mentioned that she had a new next-door neighbour, she did say that a boy my age had moved in with his grandad, but never in my wildest dreams did I think it would be Ryan – especially since Grandma described him as a "nice boy who's got lovely manners". As I'm looking at Ryan, who is currently running around squirting the backs of people's heads, I wonder if Grandma is talking about the same person.

"Ryan, outside now," Ms Morrison shouts as soon as she

walks into the classroom. Ryan drops the pipettes on the table in a massive sulk and strops outside. Ms Morrison takes off her Deputy Head's yellow high-vis and swaps it with her white lab coat. "You will all be staying behind when the bell goes for lunch, for coming into a science lab without a teacher," she declares, sitting down at her desk. My stomach lurches. I'm supposed to be meeting Zarrish by the PE changing rooms to go to athletics club at lunchtime. I've been looking at the time every two minutes since form, excitedly waiting until I can race again. I'm going to have to rush to get there on time now. I didn't even realize Ms Morrison wasn't in the room, I just followed everyone else inside.

I try my hardest to pay attention to Ms Morrison's instructions about the experiment we're about to complete, but my mind is racing with panic. I'm snapped out of my panic when Koko snatches the box of beakers and fizzy pop and plonks it on our table, causing everyone to swarm around us. Jumping out of my seat, I wait at the back for everyone to finish fighting over the equipment. I use this time to try to look at the worksheet that explains the Mentos and Soda experiment, until Koko reaches for it before me. "We don't need this," she says, scrunching it up right in front of me.

"That's the instructions," I gasp as Koko throws the paper into the recycling bin.

"Storm, this is supposed to be an experiment, so that's what we're going to do. We're going to experiment," Koko says, pulling me closer to our table.

Koko begins overfilling each beaker with fizzy pop. She's getting as much on the floor as in the beaker and I can only put my hands over my face so I don't see the disaster that is happening.

"Koko, we don't need that much," I say, peeking through the space between my fingers.

"Stop being boring," she replies, ignoring me.

"Girls, too much chatter, not enough work going on." I look at Ms Morrison with her pink goggles on and her red curls falling perfectly, then at Koko, hoping that Ms Morrison will see the cause of the disaster that is happening at our work area, but instead she points to me. "Storm, you don't seem to be doing very much, go next door for the mop and, in case you didn't guess, that's a warning for the pair of you."

I step outside the classroom and take a deep breath. It's alright for Koko. She doesn't seem to care about getting into trouble. I peer through the window into the classroom where a Year Ten class are working in silence. It would be a lot easier to walk inside if they were all talking and doing their own thing, but if I step inside now they are all going to turn round and look at me.

I walk straight past the classroom and turn round. I can do this. I put my hand forward to open the door but stop myself and take a step back. I can't do it. I can't walk in with all of those Year Tens in there. What am I going to do? I've been ages and Ms Morrison is going to be so mad when I go back, especially if I return without the mop. I think about what's worse, going into a classroom and interrupting a Year Ten lesson or going back to face an angry Ms Morrison. Neither of my options sound good.

"Why are you out here?"

I turn round to see Ryan sat down, bouncing a tennis ball against the wall. I totally forgot that Ms Morrison sent him out. That was ages ago. I wonder if she has forgotten too. He stands up and walks towards me.

"I need to get the mop."

He's staring at me in the same way that Mr Adams did when I wouldn't sit with a group for the form-time quiz. His eyes follow mine as I look back into the room full of Year Tens.

"Wait here," he says. He knocks on the door and heads straight inside.

"Thanks," I mumble as he returns with the mop. I try to

think of what to say to fill the silence. He must be thinking about how strange I am that I can't even walk into a room to get a mop.

When I get back inside, I begin cleaning up the mess, as Ms Morrison stops Ryan to give him a warning about being on his best behaviour, or else. "Koko, we already have a warning, I think we should stick to following the instructions," I plead, watching Koko reaching for more Mentos.

"Stop fretting, warnings aren't logged," she says, shrugging me off. A huge pop causes me to jump several spaces backwards. Crashing into stools that topple over like dominos, I hold my leg that's now throbbing in agony.

"Whoops!" Koko says with a half grin on her face. "Too many Mentos," she shrugs as we are both now soaked from the fizzy pop that has just exploded in front of us. I can hear my heart beating in my chest as the silence in the classroom lingers. The lunchtime bell rings but nobody dares move.

"Everyone except the two students working here can go." Ms Morrison finally breaks the silence. I look at the clock on the wall. Athletics club starts now and I'm absolutely drenched in Coca-Cola. It doesn't look like this matters, though. By the way Ms Morrison is glaring at both Koko and me, I get the feeling that we're not going to be leaving the classroom anytime soon.

The sound of a box of beakers crashing to the ground causes Ms Morrison's face to go bright red with rage. "Ryan Taylor," she says through gritted teeth. "Leave it!" she adds as Ryan starts picking the beakers up. "You only cause more trouble than good, go on, leave." I catch sight of the hurt on Ryan's face as he follows the class out.

"You two can stay in detention for the entirety of lunchtime, where you can explain why you think that it's acceptable to not follow classroom instructions. But before that, you can clean up the entire classroom." Ms Morrison walks back to her desk. "The paper towels are over there, hurry up."

I open my mouth to protest. I want to tell Ms Morrison that none of this is my fault, but the words don't come out. Instead I pick up a handful of paper towels to soak up the fizzy pop that's dripping from our table. As I go to clean up, I'm mad at Koko for getting us into this mess and even more mad at myself for not speaking up.

CHAPTER 5

"That girl is so annoying, you should put her in her place," Zarrish says. It's the end of the day and the first time I've seen Zarrish since the morning. It turns out that Zarrish didn't go to athletics club without me. After I didn't turn up, she went to the dining hall with Melissa instead. I'm relieved that she didn't go; we can start together next week.

"I wish you were in my class and then I wouldn't have these problems." I sigh. I miss being in the same class as Zarrish. In primary school we did everything together. It's only chaos without her.

She shakes her head. "I wish you were in my class. I wouldn't last two minutes in your class, especially not with Koko and Ryan." Zarrish shudders in disgust. "Don't work with Koko again. Just tell your teachers that you're not allowed to work with her. That's what I did when I didn't want to sit next to Courtney," she says.

"You're not allowed to sit next to Courtney?" I ask. I know that Zarrish and Courtney didn't really get on in primary school, but I didn't know it was that serious.

"Well, technically I am, but I couldn't spend the whole year sat next to her, so I told my teachers that Mrs Osei said we have to be kept separate in lessons," she says as if it was the easiest thing in the world to do.

"They believed you?" I ask. She shrugs. "Yeah, besides they're not going to check, are they? Not with all that marking they're always banging on about. Just tell them that Mrs Osei wants to keep you two apart. You should do it with Ryan too."

I wonder how Zarrish has it all figured out and whether I could pull off her plan. "Anyway forget about them, look what's coming up soon." She smiles, showing me an image on her phone.

"The fair!" I smile, instantly feeling better. We go to the funfair at Platt Fields Park every year. It's become a tradition. We usually eat way too much candyfloss, go on all of the rides at least twice and have a sleepover. I smile, knowing that I will always have Zarrish on my side, and think about her advice as she heads out, leaving me to wait for Isaiah.

"Storm, it was a shame you weren't in athletics club

today," Mr Harris says, walking in my direction. "Just follow me for a sec," he adds continuing to walk inside the Bistro. I follow him hesitantly, unsure if the rules still apply after school. I'm pretty sure they do.

"There is an athletics competition coming up and I want you to take part," he says handing me a letter. "This letter is for your parents to sign so you can take part in the Greater Manchester Schools Athletics Championships."

I take the letter from Mr Harris cautiously. "I've put you down for the two hundred metres and the four hundred metres. From the record you broke in PE, I know you have a real shot at winning," he says noticing my hesitation.

A lot of things are racing through my mind right now. Like, who in my year will be taking part? What will I have to do? Where will it be? Mr Harris interrupts my thoughts. "Don't worry, a few people in your year group will be taking part and some other students too. You have time to come to athletics club and practise," he says.

"Storm, there you are," Isaiah says sticking his head through the Bistro doors. He's got bags full of fabric again. Did he forget that we are getting the bus to Grandma's house today?

"Get that letter signed and bring it back to me as soon as possible," Mr Harris says as I leave to meet Isaiah. I fold the letter in half and put it in my blazer pocket before I reach him. I need time to think about this before I tell anyone. Isaiah will only tell Mum and Dad and I don't want everyone to know before I've even decided whether to do it.

"Could that be any more tragic?" Isaiah says as we turn the corner onto Grandma's street. I look up to see Mum and her friends skating in a zigzag line. Mum started a roller-skating club last year after she saw a video on YouTube. The women in the videos were glamorous and skated on a pier in California. It looks a lot different in the backstreets of Manchester.

"I can't stop!" Julie screams as she reaches for Mum. Mum holds out her hand and grabs Julie, stopping her from crashing into a pair of blue recycling bins. Mum laughs, removing her hood. They all have the same hoody on. Isaiah helped Mum design the club's logo and he used the colours of the suffragette movement because, apparently, they lived around here too.

Their laughter gets louder as we get closer.

"Hi!" Mum says as she uses the garden wall to stop herself. Julie tries to do the same but falls straight backwards and onto the ground. She cries with laughter, or pain. Possibly both. It did look like it hurt a lot.

"I'm okay," Julie whimpers as Mum and Tricia help her up.

"Make us a brew, Diane, while I rest my foot," Julie says as we watch Isaiah struggle with another bag he tries to fit through the front door.

"Isaiah, no more stuff from school," Mum says as we all follow him inside.

"Tell him not to put it in our room; it's full of his stuff already," I beg. Our room has turned into a giant maze. It's hard to find my way in and out.

"Hey, I got a text about your detention today. What's all that about?" Mum says, turning the kettle on in Grandma's kitchen, as Julie and Tricia sit down at the table.

"That wasn't my fault," I say, leaning against the kitchen door. "Koko was making a mess and I got in trouble for it as well," I explain, pointing to my shirt stained with Coca-Cola.

"Why didn't you tell your teacher that it was Koko?" Julie asks rubbing her bruised foot.

"You should have told Koko to clear it up. Do you want me to ring Mrs Osei and get it sorted?" Mum asks.

"No, don't!" I plead. That would be so embarrassing. If Mum rang in, Koko would get into trouble and then she would be even more of a pain than she is now.

"You need to stand up for yourself, Storm. Don't be so shy," Julie says.

Don't be so shy. I've heard this so many times before. As if I can just suddenly snap out of it. If only it was that easy.

As I leave Mum and her friends, Isaiah's music is already thumping through the ceiling. Dad is still at work and Grandma has her allotment friends over for a coffee evening in the living room. After Grandma gives me a slice of carrot cake and makes me say hello to her friends, which I do by putting my head round the living-room door and smiling awkwardly, I head towards the window nook in the hallway.

The window nook is cushioned and overlooks the street. It's big enough for both me and Minnie, which is good because as soon as I sit down she jumps up and lies down, resting her head on my knees. I stroke Minnie and she closes her big brown eyes. When the coast is clear, I unzip my blazer pocket and take out the letter that Mr Harris gave me. A buzz hits me as I read the letter.

Dear Parents and/or Carers of Storm Williams,
I am delighted to inform you that Storm has been selected
to take part in the Greater Manchester Schools Athletics
Championships qualifying event that will be taking place
on 15th April. Storm will take part in the two hundred

metre and four hundred metre events to qualify for the
finals, where she will have the chance to compete in her
individual events as well as to help Daisy Mill Academy
become overall champions.

The school bus will leave at 9:15 and will be back at
school for lunchtime. The qualifying event will take place
at Longford Park Stadium. Please sign the letter below,
to give Storm permission to take part in the championships.

Yours sincerely,

Mr Harris

I feel a rush of excitement as I think about racing on a real track, but then I curl up as I remember today's events. If only I'd been able to go to athletics club with Zarrish, then she would have got a letter too and I would have rushed to Mum and Dad to share the news that I am going to be racing in the athletics championships. Well, the qualifiers at least. The thought of doing it without Zarrish is too scary. It will be a lot easier if she is by my side. I'll have someone to talk to, someone to ask all the questions that I'm wondering and someone to sit next to. There is no way I can go alone. I would have to wear my PE kit to school, get on the school bus with people I don't know and stand on the starting line with everyone watching.

We have PE tomorrow. I'm sure Zarrish will see how amazing athletics is and will get a letter too. Then I can give my letter to Mum and Dad.

The door to the kitchen opens, causing me and Minnie to jump.

"So, did anything else happen at school today besides you getting a detention?" Mum asks.

I cover the letter with my hand so Mum can't see it.

"No, nothing else."

CHAPTER 6

"We're going to be late." I sigh, looking at the time.

Isaiah comes into the kitchen, pushing an old rucksack with his foot. "Can you not bring that into the kitchen? You'll get dirt all over Grandma's floors," Mum says taking a sip of her coffee before frantically waving at Minnie to stop digging up Grandma's flower bed. Isaiah ignores Mum and begins to empty old camping equipment onto the kitchen floor.

"We don't have time for this," I say, standing in the doorway with my school bag on ready to go. I wonder why everyone is still in their pyjamas when there are only twenty minutes before the morning bell rings.

"It's not my fault that I can't get in the bathroom," Isaiah says, inspecting one of his compasses.

I thought it would be a good thing that Grandma is a morning person. I thought she would help me to get Isaiah out the house on time, but it turns out it means there is another person in the queue for the bathroom. She had a lavender bath at seven this morning.

"We're practising today. We have to show Mr Harris that we can put up a tent and use all of our equipment," he says, launching into a speech about the details of his Duke of Edinburgh expedition – how he's going to be out in the wild surviving on his own with only his friends Connor and Jayden – but I've lost focus, because I can hear Dad belting out *Stop Crying Your Heart Out* by Oasis from upstairs. Mum and Isaiah find it funny but I don't.

"How can Dad take so long in the shower? He has no hair," I say putting my head down on the table and causing Mum to snort out her coffee.

"Relax, Storm. I'll ring Mrs Osei and let her know that it's not your fault that you're late today," Mum says, accepting that we're definitely going to be late to school this morning.

By the time I get to school, I'm ten minutes late to form. My bag weighs me down as I dash through the corridor. "Storm, wait up," Zarrish shouts. I stop until she catches up with me. "I'll walk you to lesson," she says reassuringly as panic doesn't leave my face.

"Are you not gonna get into trouble?" I ask. She links my arm and we continue walking.

"No, I always ask to go to the toilet to get out of form time. Mr Johnson doesn't keep a track of the time," she smiles, holding a toilet pass in her hand that explains why she isn't in form.

"You smell like a grandma," she says. I reach down to sniff my blazer. I reek of Grandma's lavender bubble bath.

"Is it really obvious?" I say. Zarrish laughs before handing me her body spray. I look round before I quickly spray myself.

"I need to tell you something," I say. I open my blazer pocket and hand her my athletics qualifier letter. She's the first person I've shown it to. "I know you would've got one if you were in PE," I say, watching her read it. "So, what do you think?"

Zarrish shrugs. "It would be good to miss lessons I guess."

"You'll definitely get a letter today after PE and then we can do it together!" I say, announcing my master plan. Zarrish is a fast runner so I know she will get a letter too. I'm so excited about athletics that, for a small moment, I forget that I'm late to form.

"Sorry Storm's late, sir," Zarrish says swinging my form-room door wide open.

"Not to worry, Storm, I got a phone call from Mrs Osei explaining that you were late to school because your dad was hogging the shower," says Mr Adams.

My face goes red as people snicker. Why on Earth would Mr Adams say that out loud? I ignore everyone as I rush to sit at my table, where Ryan is scribbling on his maths homework sheet. It looks like Koko is also doing her homework, until I look closely and notice she's actually drawing a unicorn. Ryan's muddled-up face was exactly like mine when I tried to do the homework last night. It took me ages, because I couldn't remember how to work out the area of a trapezium. When Mr Adams went through it last lesson, he asked everyone to hold up either the green card, if you understood, or the red card, if you didn't. I couldn't hold up the red card, not when everyone else held up the green one.

The bell rings for period one and I race down the corridors like lightning, excited for today's PE lesson. When I barge into the changing rooms, my excitement fades. Zarrish isn't here yet.

"Storm, do you want to come with us?" Asha asks, holding a clipboard and whistle in her hand. Asha was made a sports ambassador last term and she is taking the role very seriously. I want to stay and wait for Zarrish so I can remind her about how good it will be when we are both on the athletics team, but Miss Scott comes in and asks for an extra pair of hands to carry the equipment outside, so I have no choice but to follow them.

"Have you got your letter signed?" Mr Harris asks. I drop the bag of cones next to the benches, giving myself more time to think. I don't want to tell Mr Harris that I need to wait for Zarrish to get a letter so I can bring mine in, so I lie and say I forgot. Mr Harris tells me that I have to bring it in tomorrow and I nod before sitting down next to Koko, who is pulling out daisies from the ground.

"Storm, over here," I hear Zarrish from behind me. Butterflies rush through my stomach, except this time they feel good. It's happening! Zarrish will get a letter today. My smile immediately leaves my face when I turn round. Why is Zarrish in her school uniform?

"Hey, Storm," she says sitting down beside me.

She's going to get a kit mark. I try not to panic. So what if she forgot her kit? I wonder if she's brought her PE jumper. If she just wears something, Mr Harris will let her off like he did when I forgot my trainers. I want to ask her why she's not in her PE kit, but Mr Harris interrupts me.

"Alright, Year Seven, today we're going to be running the two hundred metres, but first, Praise and Natasha are going to lead a warm-up," Mr Harris says looking at two sixth-form students walking towards our group. The new girl, Melissa, is following behind them. Since everyone is mixed up in PE, I had hoped that she wasn't going to be in our PE class.

She isn't wearing her PE kit either, but that isn't the first thing I notice about her. She looks like she has just eaten a sour lemon as she sits down in between me and Zarrish with a massive thud.

"That Mrs Osei is such a—"

"Don't finish that sentence," Miss Scott says sternly. Melissa whispers something under her breath as Miss Scott walks away. "Why does your form have a teaching assistant, are you all stupid?" Melissa says.

"Storm isn't stupid," Zarrish says, quickly jumping to my defence. Melissa raises her eyebrow at Zarrish the same way that Mum does when we've said something wrong.

"The rest of them are though," Zarrish says smirking along with Melissa.

Melissa kisses her teeth, putting her hair into a bun before continuing to complain about how much she hates this school, even though she has been here for less than a week. She stops moaning about teachers when she spots my trainers.

"Your trainers are weird, what make are they?" she says. Mum bought me new ones when she went to Asda last night. She said there was no point going home for my old pair that were now too small for me and had holes in them anyway. Mum agreed that I could have proper branded trainers once everything at home is sorted, but until then, I will have to make do with these babyish-looking ones from the supermarket. I did hope no one would notice.

"Girls, stop talking," Mr Harris says looking directly at us. I keep my eyes firmly on the ground.

"This school, man," Melissa continues on her rant. As Mr Harris instructs us to stand up and introduces the two sixth-form students now standing at the front, I'm glad that Melissa isn't given the opportunity to continue. I don't have time for any drama right now. There is only one thing that is important today. Both Zarrish and me being on the athletics team.

"Praise and Natasha are sixth-form students who are going to be helping out in the PE department," Mr Harris explains, "and we are very lucky to have them working with us today."

Praise and Natasha wave at us with half-excited, half-nervous grins.

"Spread yourselves out," Praise says, using her arms to herd us into the correct positions. She ties up her long box-braids before nodding to Natasha to begin.

"Okay, so we are going to lead a warm-up," Natasha says flicking through her phone. "Sorry, I'm just looking for a song," she says, nervously. She walks over to the speakers

78

and plugs her phone in. The music starts blaring from the speakers. I look at Zarrish, who looks at me and smiles. Praise is blasting an old song that Zarrish and I used to dance to when she stayed at mine during the summer holidays.

"Everyone follow me," Praise shouts circling her arms around her shoulders. Everyone copies her, except for Koko, who is doing her own thing as usual. Praise and Natasha don't tell her off for not following their routine.

"Okay, now move your hips," Natasha says, still dancing as she ties up her wavy ginger hair that keeps falling in her face.

"Stop being boring, Storm," Koko says as she notices me stood still, not wanting to look silly in front of my class. Praise looks at Koko like she needs to tone down her dance moves, but she doesn't say anything. She instead looks at Natasha and laughs.

"You need to join in," Praise says to Melissa, who is also stood still. Melissa, who continues to have her arms folded, throws a dirty look towards Praise and Natasha before elbowing Zarrish to stop following along. Zarrish follows Melissa's demands and stops moving to the music.

"That's a warning for the girl at the back," Praise says, looking directly at Melissa. I step slightly away from Melissa, not wanting to get into trouble, especially since Mr Harris is watching. I want Zarrish to move forward with me so she doesn't get into trouble either, but she stays where she is. Melissa has her arms folded, looking unimpressed with Praise and Natasha.

"Don't be shy. You should be good at this," Natasha says, refocusing her attention on me, realizing that she hasn't got a chance of getting Melissa to do what she's told. "You've got that Jamaican rhythm," she grins.

"She's not Jamaican," Zarrish responds pulling me back. I can feel my face going red. The only part of my body moving are my legs but they are only quietly trembling as the other class walks out onto the field.

"She's from Barbados, like Rihanna," Koko says.

"No, she's not, her mum is from the Bahamas," Zarrish replies.

"Oh, yeah, the Bahamas. They have swimming pigs," Koko adds.

"Guys, can we focus on what we should be doing please?" Mr Harris shouts over.

"Yes, please concentrate," Natasha says.

Once everyone has finished discussing where I'm from and what it has to do with my ability to move my hips, Praise continues her routine.

"I thought this was athletics, not a dance class," I mutter to myself. I put my hand over my mouth, realizing Praise had stopped the music.

"Exactly," Melissa says, hearing my comment and wanting everyone else to hear it too. I am grateful that nobody does. "Nice one, Storm," she smirks as if I meant to be rude on purpose.

"Well done, everybody," Natasha smiles, "except for the one student who we had to give a warning to," Praise looks directly at Melissa.

As we follow Mr Harris towards the other side of the field, Melissa pulls Zarrish back to walk slower. I slow down so I can walk with them.

"It's not fair. You didn't join in," Melissa says to me. "They didn't give you a warning just because you're quiet."

Great. Melissa has only known me for five minutes and just like everyone else she has labelled me the Quiet Girl.

"They can't give warnings, they're not even teachers," Zarrish reassures Melissa.

"Warnings aren't logged anyway," Koko says coming up from behind, now wearing a daisy-chain crown on her head.

Zarrish turns to her. "Who asked you?"

My mouth opens slightly, shocked at how mean that was.

"I'm just saying." Koko shrugs.

"Yes, well stay out of other people's conversations," Zarrish snaps. I don't know what has happened with Mrs Osei and Melissa this morning, but she's in a bad mood and it's starting to rub off on Zarrish.

"Everyone go to the starting line," Mr Harris says standing next to Asha.

I stand on the starting line next to Zarrish. "This is one of the events at the qualifiers." I grin excitedly. I try to forget about my inability to shake my hips. This is what matters. I'm going to be competing in the two hundred metres at the qualifying event. I need to see if I can do this.

Asha is at the side of the track with her whistle ready. "Stand behind the white line," she bellows across the field. I don't know how someone so tiny can have such a loud voice. Everyone shuffles backwards and awaits her instructions.

"This is so dead," Melissa mutters.

"I'm expecting you to be super fast with your trainers on now!" Mr Harris smiles towards me.

"Not with those trainers on," Melissa snickers.

I pretend that I don't hear her as Asha orders us into position.

"On your marks. Get set. GO!"

I jump off the starting line but Melissa pulls my shirt so

I jolt backwards. "This is boring. Let's go inside," she says waving over to Mr Harris.

"Girls, why aren't you running?" Mr Harris asks.

"I hurt my foot when we were warming up," Melissa says stumbling off the track. I follow her unwillingly, watching the rest of the class whizz down the track.

"We can't go inside. What about the qualifier?" I whisper to Zarrish, trying to get her to remember that she needs to join in if she's going to get a letter too.

"Forget about the qualifier thing. Melissa is right, this is boring. Come on, we can chill inside," she says.

"Well alright, but it doesn't need three of you. Zarrish can take Melissa to the medical room," Mr Harris says, believing Melissa's fake injury. "Storm, you go back to the starting line, we're about to race again."

Mr Harris claps to the others to head back over. I walk back to the starting line with my master plan of getting Zarrish on the athletics team falling apart. This time, Mr Harris puts us into groups of eight, with each of us taking one lane. My group is up first and as Mr Harris ushers me into lane four, I can't help but look at the rest of the class watching in anticipation.

"We're going to smash this," Teija says standing in lane five, still on a high from winning the first race. I only just manage to smile back, not quite matching her level of confidence.

"Focus on your own lane," Mr Harris shouts from the sidelines, signalling for Asha to start the race. She nods and gets ready to blow her whistle.

I try to refocus my mind on the track in front of me.

"On your marks. Get set. Go!"

I leap off the starting line and push forward as fast as my legs can take me. I overtake most girls, until I'm out in front. Like a rocket, Teija shoots past me just as I turn round to see who's close. *Keep going,* I tell myself, striding forward.

I edge closer until we're shoulder to shoulder. My legs are tiring but the end is too close to give up now. Using all of the energy I have left, I leap across the finish line.

"Yo, you beat me again!" Teija says as I drop to the ground to catch my breath. For a second, I think she is mad at me for winning but she breaks into a smile – reaching out her arm to pull me up.

"Teija, over here!" Maya shouts, crossing the finish line. Teija leaves me to join her friends and suddenly I'm alone, watching everyone break off into small groups to chat. I twiddle my hair; unsure what to do with myself.

"You are going to be a force to be reckoned with," says Miss Scott walking over to me. "You're allowed to big yourself up; you were amazing. You should be proud of yourself," she says, noticing how deflated I feel.

No matter how big the thrill of racing just felt, I can't do this by myself. I need Zarrish to be a force to be reckoned with too. When Mr Harris dismisses us, I get changed quickly to meet Zarrish. She is standing by the PE steps with Melissa, who has an ice pack on her foot.

"Wait, you did have your PE kit?" I look at Zarrish's green gym bag across her shoulder.

"Melissa didn't have hers so she asked if I wouldn't wear mine. She didn't want to be on her own," she says.

I tense up in frustration. Zarrish knew that I wanted her to get a qualifying letter, yet she still chose to not wear her kit.

"You're not mad are you?" Zarrish says. Melissa looks on with a raised eyebrow.

"No, course not," I lie, not wanting any drama.

"You two, don't move from those steps. You're both writing kit lines at break," Mr Harris says, pointing to both Melissa and Zarrish as he walks into his office.

"Hold up," Melissa says looking from her phone. "*Lines?*"

Zarrish nods. "That's the punishment when you forget your kit. You have to write *I will remember to bring in my PE kit* eighty times." Melissa's face drops and I try not to laugh at her reaction.

"Stuff that," she snorts throwing her ice pack in the bin by the PE office doors. She peers down the corridor to see who's there. "Quick, leg it," she says, escaping out of the PE doors five minutes before the bell is supposed to go.

Oh, so now she wants to run.

CHAPTER 7

Mum and Dad are both in Grandma's kitchen when I get home from school. I listen to their conversation as I pour myself a glass of lemonade, drinking it slowly so I have a reason to eavesdrop. But their conversation about "insurance", "builders" and "contracts" doesn't make much sense. I can tell by the way that Mum is clicking her pen frantically, and by the way that Dad is losing his phone voice and sounding more Mancunian by the minute, that whatever they're talking about isn't good.

I'm washing my glass and putting it on the draining board when Dad bangs on the table to get my attention. With one hand still holding the phone pressed to his ear as he utters "Mmh" every so often, he waves his other arm frantically. His whole body jolts sideways as if we're playing a game of charades. Mum joins me in looking at him with utter confusion, until something out of the window catches my eye. Minnie is currently digging a hole worthy of a World-War-One battlefield. I open the back door and Minnie stands upright. Her tongue is sticking out lopsided, looking pleased at her achievement of digging up half of Grandma's garden. Grandma has book club tonight, which is good because I dread to imagine her reaction when she sees this. Minnie is ready to play chase but I call her bluff. I pretend to go left, causing her to go right and I catch her just before she takes off. I bring her inside and her paws leave a muddy trail behind. Mum looks like she has lost the will to live, so I hurriedly try to find the wet wipes to clean Minnie's paws but I have no idea where Grandma keeps them.

I give up in defeat, pointing to Minnie's lead to tell Mum and Dad that I'm taking her for a walk.

When I finally step outside, I stop immediately. Ryan is sat on his garden wall. As soon as Minnie and Ryan collide, I know there is going to be trouble. Minnie has already decided which way we're walking to the park and drags me forward, so I have no choice but to walk in the direction of Ryan. I expect him to look up, but he doesn't. We walk straight past him and he doesn't even notice us. No excitement, no wanting to hold Minnie, no annoying comments. Nothing. I turn my head round to see what he's doing and he's in the same position. Head down, kicking stones with his shoe. Should I say something? I decide against it and carry on walking.

My phone pings. It's Mum telling me not to be too long since it's starting to rain. I lift up my hood as the rain starts to fall heavier and I decide to scroll through my phone. There is a photo of the athletics club on the school's social page. It's from the other day when I missed going to club because I had a detention with Koko. I quickly scroll past it, trying not to look at everyone in the photo smiling as they hold up their hands in the number one position. I keep on scrolling, unable to shake off the disappointment that I wasn't there, until I freeze. Zarrish put up a photo of her and Melissa sixteen minutes ago. They are both still in their school uniforms, but it doesn't look like the photo was taken at school. From the ice-cream sundaes they're holding, it looks like they are at the dessert shop in Didsbury. The one that Zarrish and I go to when I stay over at hers. It's weird to see them together out of school. *Why wasn't I invited?* I wonder as I put my phone away and dash home as the rain lashes down, bumping into Grandma as she arrives home from book club.

"It's the same every week," Grandma says as we walk back inside with Minnie. Minnie shakes the water from her fur, causing Grandma to squeal. Ryan was still sat on his garden wall when I ran back home with Minnie. He doesn't seem bothered that it's pouring down with rain. Both Grandma and I watch as his grandad, who is taller than I expected considering Ryan is so small, tries to get him inside.

"He sits on that wall waiting for his mum to pick him up. Sometimes she's on time, sometimes she's late and more often than not she never comes at all." Grandma explains that Ryan is supposed to have contact with his mum every week. I can't imagine only seeing my parents once a week, in a room with a supervisor watching our every move. I turn back to look at Ryan, suddenly feeling anxious for him.

A rummaging sound from the top of the stairs causes Minnie to leap back into her excited self. "I need Dad's toolbox," Isaiah shouts, jumping down the stairs.

"For what? Actually, don't tell me. I don't want to know," Mum says, walking into the living room. Mum usually goes to Zumba at the community centre tonight. She never misses it. But the look on her face as she shuffles through paperwork suggests that she isn't going anywhere, and as I look out of the window again to see Ryan walking back into his grandad's house, it looks like he isn't either.

"Ew, that's gross!" I yelp walking into the bedroom that I

have to share with Isaiah. I look under my feet to find a plate of leftover egg fried rice now squashed into my socks. I quickly take them off and give the plate to Isaiah, who seamlessly puts it back on the floor before returning to do his school work.

"You're so annoying," he says as I take one of his sweaty T-shirts, that is now on my side of the bedroom, and throw it towards him. It lands on his head and he chucks it onto the mountain of his belongings that are now in a heap on the floor.

"Can you not see this mess?" I ask, pointing to every corner of the room. Honestly, how can one boy have this much stuff?

"It looks fine to me." He shrugs, continuing to follow instructions on a YouTube video while fiddling with lights on a circuit board.

Mum and Dad haven't stopped talking about our house in hushed, worried tones all evening, so I fight the urge to run downstairs to complain about Isaiah. Instead, I turn off the lights and shuffle into bed. I try my best to fall asleep, saving my "I can't survive another night of Isaiah" speech for the morning.

"Oh yeah, Mr Harris told me to remind you to bring in your letter for the athletics qualifier," Isaiah says. I open my eyes immediately. I didn't want Isaiah finding out because he will only tell Mum and Dad and now Zarrish isn't doing it, there's no point.

"I'm not going to hand it in," I say.

"Why not?" he asks.

"Because Zarrish isn't going and I'm not doing it by myself," I admit. There is no way Zarrish is going to get a letter after today's PE lesson and, even if she did, she wouldn't do it. She made it crystal clear that she wasn't bothered about athletics.

"What would you have to do if you did take part?" he says, not dropping the conversation.

Isaiah turns the light back on and I sit up to explain to him what Mr Harris told me when he gave me the letter. I've been selected to compete in the Greater Manchester Schools Athletics Championships. The first event is the qualifying event where I would be running the two hundred metres and four hundred metres. If I finish my race in the top three, I will move on to the next stage, which is the finals. Making it to the finals is not only important because you have a chance to win a medal in your races, but the school with the most medals becomes overall champion, meaning we can win a trophy as a team too. A tidal wave of excitement hits me as I imagine myself stepping out onto the springy floors of a real athletics track. I turn the light back off and slump back in my bed, knowing that I won't be competing because I'm too scared to do it without Zarrish.

"Mr Harris told me that you're the fastest Year Seven in years. You should go for it," Isaiah says, switching the light back on.

I huff and get up from under my duvet to turn the light back off. "I can't do it without Zarrish. I'll be on my own. It'll be too awkward," I explain, just as Isaiah turns the light back on.

"I'm trying to sleep," I protest, turning the light back off. I stumble to the ground after tripping over his GCSE art coursework that hasn't quite dried yet. "Isaiah!" I shout, my pyjamas now covered in PVA glue.

"It's only 9:30, besides I need to get this finished – Mrs Osei is expecting me to have her fashion show outfit done by the end of the week," he says.

I sigh. "I guess that's the difference between you and me. You're Mr Perfect. Everyone expects you to be the best at everything. At least no one will care if I don't enter the championships." I reach over to the light switch once more, using cushions as stepping stones to avoid any more of Isaiah's mess on the floor.

"Oi, you two, are you having a disco with those lights?"

Mum shouts from the landing.

"Tell Isaiah!" I yell.

"Tell Storm!" Isaiah yells, turning the light back on.

"I'm telling both of you!" Mum says sternly.

Isaiah asks to see the letter, so I get up and take it out of my blazer pocket before quickly turning the light back off. I hear Isaiah huff and he turns round looking back at the screen of his laptop that is glaring brightly.

"Yes!!!"

With the lights on his circuit board now flashing on and off, he makes me jump as he leaps up out of his chair to celebrate, like he's just scored a winning goal at Old Trafford.

"What? You've got to celebrate your own wins," he says, echoing what Miss Scott said to me earlier in PE.

"One way you can celebrate your win in PE is by competing in the championships," Isaiah says sitting back down, his lights flickering like Blackpool Illuminations.

"Absolutely not going to happen," I say. "And don't even think about telling Mum and Dad," I warn.

"You need to stop caring about what other people think. Stop being so shy," Isaiah says.

I roll over on my side and pull my duvet over me in frustration. When I stepped through the school gates on my first day at Daisy Mill, I thought maybe this was my fresh start. Maybe I could be myself here, without worrying whether people are going to like me. I had it all planned. I was going to start Year Seven with a bang. No more hiding. I was going to be involved in everything, just like Isaiah. I thought I was ready, but as soon as Mr Adams made us stand up and share three facts about ourselves during our first ever form time, I froze. From then on I knew things would just be the same as before. Isaiah wouldn't understand. It would be no big deal for Isaiah to take part in the championships. He would do it with sass and confidence. I could never do that.

"Isaiah!" I shout as the bright light interrupts my flashback.

"Two more minutes!" he says as I reach for a pillow to chuck at him. I resist and lift my duvet over my head again, trying my hardest to push the championships out of my mind.

CHAPTER 8

"Sorry, it just slipped out!"

It's the next day and I'm walking with Zarrish to find a spot in the corridor to sit in during lunchtime. The dining hall is way too crowded and it's raining too much to go outside. I put my cheese and tomato pizza slice back in its plastic wrapper, suddenly not feeling hungry any more. I'm finding it hard to forgive Zarrish for what she has just told me. She invited Melissa to the fair; something that we have done just the two of us since the beginning of time.

"I know you've been made her buddy and everything," I sigh as we sit down. "But why did you have to invite her to the fair?"

I know it sounds mean and I don't like saying it, but first Melissa gets me in trouble with Mr Peterson, then she causes a scene in PE and then she gets us in *more* trouble for legging it. Now she's invited to the fair? Zarrish was only supposed to show Melissa round the school and help her settle in. Well, she's done that, so why is Melissa hanging around?

"Melissa isn't my buddy any more. She's my friend. Just give her a chance, I know you'll get on. You'll like her."

I look at her doubtfully and she tries to laugh away my doubts.

"Where is she anyway?" I ask.

"She had to stay behind for talking back to Mr Adams during our maths lesson."

Of course, the reason she's in trouble is because she was talking back. Melissa is full of attitude and I don't understand why Zarrish likes her. But she does, so I will try my best to become friends with her too. I think about asking Zarrish about the photo I saw of her and Melissa last night. She did put it on her social so she must know I saw it. She hasn't mentioned it though. So maybe I shouldn't either.

"Girls, please move from the corridor," Ms Morrison says as she walks past with Ryan several steps behind her. He's dragging his bag across the floor in no rush to keep up with Ms Morrison, who is already round the corner. "Ryan Taylor, you'd best still be behind me," her voice echoes.

"I am," Ryan mumbles.

"I wonder what he's done," I whisper, hoping he can't hear me.

"Probably something stupid, as always," Zarrish says.

"I actually felt sorry for him yesterday. He was waiting for his mum outside his grandad's house for ages and she never turned up."

"Would you?" she says, giving Ryan a dirty look as he finally turns the corner.

"Zarrish!" I say a little too loudly.

"What? I'm only saying," she scoffs. "He's a nightmare."

"My grandma said his mum hardly ever shows up and he is left waiting for ages every week until he gives up," I say. Zarrish is right, Ryan can be a nightmare. But no one deserves to be stood up, especially by their mum.

I feel a pang of regret speaking about Ryan behind his back. I mean, it's not a secret that he lives with his grandad. I don't think it is anyway. It's not like it's a big deal. Zarrish wouldn't say anything to anyone anyway. She's not mean like that.

Zarrish's phone buzzes and I take a bite out of my pizza. "Melissa says meet her in the dining hall," she says, quickly pulling me back up. As we walk down the corridor, I can see Melissa waiting by the windows. She's saying hi to just about everyone who walks past her. How does she know this many people already? She's only just got here.

"This song is a TUNE!"

Music starts blaring from Melissa's phone. She doesn't seem to care that it's loud enough for everyone else to hear. "We should add it to our fair playlist," Melissa says.

I turn to look at Zarrish. Fair playlist? Since when do we have a fair playlist? I don't know the song blaring out, so I try my hardest to think about something to say to join in with their excitement.

"The fair is going to be so good, I'm glad you're coming," I say to Melissa with a smile.

"Innit," Zarrish says, nudging me as she acknowledges my efforts. I watch as Melissa lifts up my slice of pizza, takes a bite and then puts it back in place again. I look round to see if Zarrish noticed, but she didn't.

"We all have to dress up," Melissa says still chewing my pizza.

"Dress up?" I wince.

"Do your make-up like this," Zarrish says, showing me the screen on her phone. The girl on the screen is wearing a face full of make-up. She also looks way older than us.

"I don't have that much make-up," I say. I don't have any make-up really, only a couple of lip glosses and an eyeshadow palette that I got for my birthday but have never used.

"Well get some then, or you won't be in our photos.

You'll ruin the aesthetics," Melissa snaps.

I turn to Zarrish for help. "I can help you do your make-up before we go," she says, taking back her phone. Melissa's eyes widen like she has just thought of a brilliant idea.

"I'm not being rude, but you could do with a makeover and you're in luck because I am so good at giving them," Melissa says, looking at me.

"Lesson please, girls," Miss Scott calls as she walks past just as the bell rings for period five.

"She can't tell us what to do," Melissa sneers, giving Miss Scott a look. "What?" Melissa says, looking at me. I shrug, not answering. I guess I look confused as to why she is always so intent on getting into trouble.

"I can make you look better right now," she says, steering the conversation back to the makeover.

"The bell has just gone," I say, putting my bag on my shoulder. I have maths now and it's right on the other side of the building.

"Don't be so boring," Melissa says, pulling me into the girls' toilets, before demanding that I take my blazer off and tie it round my waist.

"Ouch," I yelp as she pulls out my hair from my side plait and shoves it into a high bun.

"See," she says to Zarrish as they both approve my new

look. I try my best not to look in the mirror so I don't see my new hairstyle, but Melissa pulls my face towards the mirror giving me no choice.

"Don't ruin it, your hair looks nice for once," she says, slapping my hand down as I try to reach up to undo the tight bun.

"Let's walk Storm to lesson," Zarrish says as I look at her helplessly.

"Good idea. The later we get to science, the better," Melissa agrees, putting her lip gloss on as she looks in the mirror. I quickly untie my school blazer from round my waist while I follow them out of the toilets and into the corridor.

"Hey, Storm, you coming to maths?" Koko says, noticing us as she skips past showing no worry about being late.

"Ew, we're having a private conversation," Zarrish snaps. Koko shrugs, walking away.

I look at Zarrish in shock at her meanness.

"What's up with you? We don't like Koko, remember?" Zarrish says to me. I tug the fastenings on my bag. Yeah, Koko always gets me in trouble but Zarrish is making it her mission to be mean to her.

"Forget about that loser," Melissa says, pushing her way in the middle of Zarrish and me before linking her arm into mine. "Just stick with me, Storm, and you'll be alright." I smile but my smile fades as soon as Melissa looks away.

I don't feel alright. Sticking with her doesn't seem like a good idea, but as she links Zarrish's arm it seems like I don't have a choice.

I jolt backwards as Melissa turns round quickly at the sight of Mr Harris walking in our direction.

"Storm!"

Mr Harris is calling me, but Melissa holds onto my arm tight as we walk faster down the corridor. "Ignore him, he probably wants to shout at us for being late to lesson," Zarrish says, still sour from PE. My name is echoed down the corridor again. "I better stop," I say, managing to release my arm from Melissa.

"Alright, goody two shoes," Melissa scowls, pulling Zarrish along until they scarper down the corridor leaving me alone. I gulp as I turn to face Mr Harris, who manages to catch up with me.

"I have your letter for the athletics qualifier. Make sure you come to athletics club next week to start training with the team."

There is a moment of silence as I stand in confusion. I didn't give my letter back to Mr Harris. I haven't even shown it to Mum and Dad. The last person to have it was Isaiah.

Isaiah.

I am going to kill him.

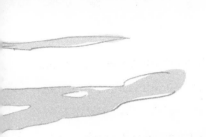

CHAPTER 9

"He was only looking out for you, Storm."

I'm in Grandma's kitchen. I rushed home to tell Mum and Dad that Isaiah handed in my qualifying letter without me knowing, but it seems that Mum and Dad are both on his side.

"Storm, you should've told us yourself. From what I can gather from Isaiah, this is huge!" Dad says, trying to make me feel better but it's not working. Why is no one seeing my side?

"You don't understand. Zarrish isn't doing it and I can't go by myself," I say, trying to explain why I absolutely can't do this. I sit down at the table opposite Mum, who has just got home from her roller-skating club.

"Of course you can do it by yourself. You don't always need to be with Zarrish," she says.

"You've managed to be in a form group without Zarrish, so you can manage this," Dad adds. I grimace. If only they could see me struggle to give answers in the weekly form quiz, or trip over my words when reading in English, then maybe they would understand just how much I'm not managing in my form group.

"Besides," Grandma says, joining the conversation. She's sitting beside Mum, keeping one eye on Minnie, who is eyeing up her flower beds in the garden. "You did mention that you're the fastest in Year Seven. You shouldn't waste your talent."

I shake my head, deflated.

Why is Isaiah banging on about this to everyone? Who else has he told?

Mum and Dad both shake their heads in agreement. "You can do it, Storm," Mum says. "And to celebrate, it's family night and we're going bowling!" Dad smiles.

"Do I have to come?" Isaiah says, walking into the kitchen, not looking up from his laptop.

Isaiah doesn't seem to care that I'm mad at him. In fact, the only thing he says about it is that I should be pleased that I've been selected to be on the athletics team, especially since his friend Jayden has been going to athletics club since it started and still didn't get a letter to compete.

"Are you a part of this family?" Dad asks. Isaiah kisses his teeth, which makes Dad cross. He hates it when he does that.

"I have a life, you know," Isaiah says, closing the lid of his laptop.

"I'm glad to hear it," Dad says, grabbing his keys from the table.

"I don't have to come, do I?" Grandma asks.

"Well, you could stay here and look after Minnie," Dad suggests, opening the kitchen door to let Minnie in.

"I'll fetch my jacket," Grandma says, standing up quickly and nudging Isaiah to do the same.

"Come on, Williams family night needs every single Williams, so grab your coat and a positive attitude and let's go have some fun," Dad chants, ushering us out of the kitchen.

I start to walk to the car but Dad stops me. "We're getting the tram."

My face drops. "What? Why?" I groan.

"Because parking in town is too expensive," Mum says.

"Plus, I thought you two wanted to save the planet?" she asks. Isaiah and I look at each other and groan. One time Isaiah suggested having a meat-free day to help the environment, after hearing Ms Morrison's assembly on global warming, and Mum and Dad use it against us every chance they get.

The tram stop is full when we reach it and we stand back as one stops and people pile on. Dad puts his card on the machine and gets out five tickets.

"I love this song," Dad says, bouncing up and down to the sound of the busker who is playing a tune on his guitar.

"Dad. Stop," I say, but he jiggles even more until it turns into a dance. Instead of telling him to stop, Mum joins in too.

"Don't look at me. Once they start you can't stop them," Grandma says, rolling her eyes but smiling at the same time.

"I'm with Storm on this one. You two look like fools," Isaiah says, moving closer to me and Grandma.

"Did you hear that, Dave? Our own child, who we brought into this world, just called us fools," Mum says, twirling round as she continues to dance round the tram stop. A few people are watching. Two university students dressed in pyjamas are smiling and by the way they are holding their phones, I'm pretty sure they're secretly recording.

"I guess fools can't buy food from Nando's," Dad says doing air guitar.

"Nah, I didn't say that," Isaiah says. Another tram comes towards us and Mum and Dad both stop dancing to get on.

We arrive at the bowling alley five minutes late. There's hardly anyone here so the man behind the ticket counter doesn't seem to mind.

"Do we not need to change our shoes?" Dad asks.

"Dad, this isn't the nineties. Nobody does that any more," Isaiah says, as we walk past the arcade games and to the bowling alley. Grandma follows Mum to order nachos as we sit down.

"Enter my name as Winner," Isaiah says to Dad as he puts in our names on the screen.

"Don't be a weirdo," I say. Honestly, sometimes Isaiah really does the most.

"Right, Storm. Youngest first."

I get up and pick a bowling ball. They're all heavy. I pick up the pink ball and lift my arm backwards and watch the ball glide down the line and straight into the gutters.

"Unlucky," Isaiah says reaching for a handful of the nachos that Mum puts down on the table.

"Yes!" Dad says, doing a victory dance as he gets a strike. He does this every time. Isaiah is up next. He too gets a strike and copies Dad's dance. He sits back down and smiles.

"Oh, look who is enjoying himself," Mum laughs.

"Can you all enjoy yourselves without being totally embarrassing?" I mutter, looking around the bowling alley that has suddenly got more crowded.

"Oh shut up, Storm. Don't be so boring," Isaiah says, grabbing a handful of nachos. His words hit me hard.

"I'm not boring!" I say, throwing a nacho at him. His comments wouldn't usually get to me, but I'm sick of people thinking I'm boring just because I'm quiet. Maybe that's why Zarrish went out without me. Maybe she finds Melissa cooler than me. That's one of the reasons why I don't want to go to athletics club on my own. Nobody will speak to me because they'll think I'm boring too. I'll be on my own. Melissa has been at Daisy Mill for five minutes and she has already made friends with everyone. Maybe if I was more like Melissa I could go to athletics club without being totally awkward.

Maybe I don't need Zarrish next to me, maybe I just need to be more like her and Melissa and that way I will find it easier to join in.

I stand up to bowl. I hold the ball and release it down the bowling lane.

Strike.

CHAPTER 10

"Tell a joke."

I'm sat at Grandma's kitchen table waiting for Isaiah to finish sewing feathers onto Ms Morrison's outfit for the fashion show. Because Isaiah handed in my letter, I have to go to athletics club after school today and since Zarrish has made it clear that she isn't interested in running, I have to go alone.

"Good idea," Mum says, agreeing with Dad. Mum and Dad have been trying to give me tips on how to feel less awkward around new people when I go to athletics club.

"Here, listen to this, how do you stop an astronaut's baby from crying? You rocket!" Dad says, almost snorting out his coffee.

"Wait, here's one. What do you call a fake noodle? An..." Mum's laughter at her own joke stops her from continuing.

"An...an impasta," she finally manages to get out.

"See, it works! You're laughing," Dad points at me.

"I'm not laughing because it's funny, I'm laughing because you two are ridiculous." There is absolutely no way that I am going to walk into athletics club and tell everyone Mum and Dad's jokes.

"Just be yourself, Storm," Mum says, managing to recover from her joke. I don't tell Mum that being myself is the problem. She stands up to let Minnie into the garden. She only got in from her shift three hours ago. She sits back down at the table with her dressing gown on that makes her look like a giant polar bear. Dad hands her a coffee before sitting down too. Isaiah joins us from upstairs and we all stare at him as he eats a bowl of cornflakes mixed with golden syrup and chocolate chips.

"What?" he says as we all look at him in disgust. "You can enjoy life, you know."

Mum shakes her head, laughing, before getting up to let Minnie back in.

"Do you want to go?" Dad asks, steering the conversation back to athletics club.

Of course I want to go. Running is the first thing I've liked since starting at Daisy Mill. The first thing that I'm good at.

"Yes I do, but I won't know anyone there," I say. Athletics

club has been on since the beginning of term. From the photo I saw on the school's social page, everyone already knows each other.

"Isaiah can always go with you," Mum suggests. I put my head on the kitchen table with a groan. Having Isaiah walking me in would be so embarrassing. I can't imagine anyone else needing their big brother to take them.

I remember my plan. I can't go as myself. I have to go as Melissa. Cool, confident and able to fit in straight away.

"Just think of it this way: by the end of the day you'll have been to athletics club and you'll be sat here saying how much fun it was," Dad says, trying to reassure me. I try not to think that far ahead.

I'm sweating and I'm not sure if it's because I'm nervous about athletics club starting in five minutes, or because Ms Morrison has the radiators on full blast and won't open the windows. Unlike Ryan, who has had his head on the desk ever since Ms Morrison gave him a detention (for smacking Abdul over the head with a textbook at the beginning of the lesson) I've been checking the time on the clock every two minutes. I've been trying to answer the questions, but half of Ryan's head has been lying on page thirty-seven, which has the diagram of the solar system on it, so I've just had to guess half my answers. Detentions are supposed to make you change your behaviour, but for Ryan it just stops him completely. Once he has been given a detention, that's it. He's done. Ms Morrison hasn't even tried to get him to do anything and she's looked over at our table at least three times. Miss Scott tried to get him to do some work but Ms Morrison told her to leave him. Then she whispered something to her before going to help Koko, who was too busy doodling to focus on answering the questions.

"Right, Year Seven, please pay attention," Ms Morrison says, stopping the class from packing away at the sound of the end-of-day bell. She clicks the remote on the board to reveal a new slide that says "Homework Project – Pair Work".

Pair work? I join my class in an echo of groans.

Ms Morrison doesn't ask the class to be quiet, she just sips her coffee and waits.

"It's fine. We can stay here for as long as it takes," Ms Morrison says.

"Doesn't bother me, I've got a detention anyway." Ryan shrugs, finally lifting his head.

I look at the time and bite my nails. The bustle of other students on the corridors makes everyone go silent.

"You will be working with the person next to you to create a model of the solar system. You have six weeks to complete your project. Nobody is leaving until everyone has written it down in their planner," Ms Morrison says, as the corridors suddenly become flooded with people. I quickly scribble in my planner. I can't be late for athletics club; I can't walk in when it's already started. Everyone will be looking at me. I shove everything in my bag and put my chair on the table. Ms Morrison is standing at the door waiting to escort Ryan to detention. He closes his book slowly and reaches for his planner in his blazer pocket.

"Come on, man," Abdul says to Ryan, who we are all waiting for. Ryan cracks his knuckles and writes his homework down slowly.

"Can we go, Ms Morrison? This isn't fair," Koko says, edging herself closer to the door.

"No one is leaving until everyone is ready. You know the rules by now."

We all know the rules. Ms Morrison reminds us every lesson. Ryan knows that none of us can go until he's ready. Why is he doing this? Abdul complains that he has to get the bus, Koko informs the class that she needs to get to drama club and Jack has to get his little sister from primary school on his way home. None of this is making Ryan go any faster.

The whole class watches as Ryan stands up and tucks his chair under the table.

"On the table!" the whole class shouts in unison. The smirk on Ryan's face makes the room even more cross and after Ryan receives threats from Abdul and Jack, Ms Morrison has had enough. She tells Ryan to leave immediately. He follows her out and pushes a chair off the table as he leaves. When we're finally out of the classroom, I'm already five minutes late to athletics club.

I run towards PE, quickly throwing on my jumper and leggings once I reach the changing room, before squeezing my feet into my old trainers. I begged Mum to go back home to find them. She didn't understand why I wanted my old trainers that have holes in the bottom, but Melissa said it is better to wear branded trainers than the ones Mum bought me from the supermarket, even if it means getting my socks soaked from the wet grass. By the time I make it to the field, I'm even more hot and bothered than before.

Groups of people are dotted around the field. I'm not sure which way to turn. Some are running, some are huddled round the long jump and a few are practising the hurdles. I can't see Mr Harris or any other teacher anywhere. My feet remain glued to the ground in the middle of the field as I think about what to do. I try my best to fight the tears that

I can feel filling my eyes, because I shouldn't be crying over something like this and I don't want to start crying in the middle of the school field.

"Storm?"

Mr Harris walks out of the PE office just as I turn back towards the changing rooms. "Have you not made it out onto the field yet?" he asks. He doesn't give me time to explain. "Danielle is just walking out now too. Danielle, can you take Storm to warm up?" he asks a girl with red braids that go all the way down to her waist. She nods and leads me back outside to the field. I follow Danielle, who starts jogging. I try to stay close to her as we pass the Year Nine football team, who are playing on the Astroturf, and the photography club, who are taking photographs of the trees in blossom near the library building.

"Are you Isaiah's little sister?" Danielle asks. "You have the same freckles," she points out. "I'm Danielle," she smiles. I don't know how she can talk and jog at the same time because I am struggling.

As we get back to Mr Harris, who is standing by the edge of the track now, she's already told me everyone's names. There are Edie and Razan, two Year Eights who turn up every session and win everything. Aaron, Prince and Bobby, the Year Nine boys who don't turn up every session and still win their races. Then there are the Year Tens alongside Danielle – Mila, Fraser and Lily – and the Year Elevens, Jayden, Aisha and Dylan. I am one of three Year Sevens, along with Teija and Rico.

Mr Harris splits us into teams to practise racing for the qualifiers. I go with Edie, Razan, Aaron and Rico to an empty section of the track. Rico suggests that I line up to race Edie and Razan in a two-hundred-metre sprint.

He shouts from the sidelines: "On your marks. Get set. Go."

I jump off the starting line. I get distracted, as I notice Ryan is sat on a bench with Ms Morrison, refusing to go inside the main hall for detention. Ryan has been refusing to go to detentions lately. He is one more incident away from going on the yellow report. Only a handful of people are on the yellow report, because it's described as a last resort. If you mess up when on the yellow report then you're out of Daisy Mill for good.

Edie and Razan both beat me as I cross the finish line in last place. "Good race," Edie high-fives Razan and I follow glumly behind them as we walk back over to everyone.

"Storm, come over here for a sec," Mr Harris shouts from the sidelines. "Stop looking around you. It slows you down. Keep your shoulders down and your head looking straight in front. Focus on your own lane."

I take his advice and head back to the starting line, trying to hide my discomfort from having wet socks and squashed toes. This time Teija has joined our group and my hands feel clammy as she stands next to me on the track, ready to race.

Rico is ready to count us down again. "On your marks. Get set. Go."

I leap off the starting line. I do what Mr Harris tells me to do. I don't look left, I don't look right. I just focus on my own lane. The thrill of running makes me leap through the finish line. Then I stumble over unable to slow myself down. I don't feel as embarrassed as usual, though, because I can hear Mr Harris shouting from the other end of the track.

"That was quality! Absolute quality!"

I won. Rico reaches for a high five and soon I'm high-fiving everyone. The whistle signals for the end of practice and I'm shocked at how fast it went. "Come on," Edie says, running back over to the group now huddled on the ground near Mr Harris. I join the rest of the group, who sit down in silence as we devour the ice pops Mr Harris hands out. I guess coming to athletics club wasn't so scary after all.

"Yo, Isaiah's little sister is rapid!" Danielle says, striding over and grabbing a strawberry ice pop.

Mr Harris says the words I can't manage to say, "Her name is Storm."

CHAPTER 11

"Are you sure that you trained this dog?" Grandma shouts, opening the kitchen door. Minnie leaps into the garden with yellow and blue paint splattered across her face. "She's ruined my painting." Grandma frowns. She puts the canvas on the garden table and leans it against the wall before taking a step back to look at it. I join her in staring at the painting of a city landscape, with paw prints now sprawled across the skyline.

It's Saturday and I've been out in the garden practising for the athletics qualifier that's coming up next week. After athletics club, I wrote down a list of things that I need to work on to improve my running technique. I've spent all morning running up and down Grandma's garden, trying to practise pushing my knees up while swinging my arms back and forward as I run.

"It looks like one of those modern paintings," Mum says, coming out into the garden. She's trying to make Grandma feel better but it's not working. Grandma picks up her canvas and puts it in the bin. Dad did take Minnie to training when she was a puppy, but the old lady who ran the class banned Minnie after she proved that her catchphrase, "*I can train any dog, any size, any issue*," was clearly untrue.

"We're going out in a few minutes and we'll take the dog," Mum says apologetically.

Since Grandma's garden is small and now covered in Minnie-sized holes, I asked Mum if we could go to the park so I can practise properly. Mum did want to go on her roller skates but I told her that would be cheating, not to mention totally embarrassing.

We're at Alexandra Park for less than five minutes before Mum gets stopped by someone she knows from her roller-skating club. I look round the park. It's still early so it's not too busy, thankfully. There is an exercise group warming up near the duck pond and a pair of elderly men are playing dominos on a table near the cafe. Besides that, the park is empty. I stand and wait patiently for Mum to stop chatting. Mum asks about how someone's daughter is getting on at university and whether someone's dad is doing well after spending a week in hospital. She laughs loudly at something she missed in the last Zumba class, but speaks in a hushed tone when they ask about our house. The mention of our house seems to make the conversation come to an abrupt end and Mum signals that it's time for us to be getting on.

"Why didn't you want to talk about the house? Has something else happened?" I ask Mum as her friend walks away.

"I didn't want to bore her with talk of building work. Nothing has happened," she says before picking up a jogging pace, Minnie running in excited circles around us. "Now come on, I thought we were practising for a race."

Mum ends the conversation and I have no choice but to start jogging after her. "You were always so fast when you were little. Mind you, usually you were running in the opposite direction to where you were supposed to be going." I give Mum a side eye but smile, because I know it's true. I remember running after Mum when she dropped me off at nursery for the first time and running out of holiday club, not wanting to stay alone when we went to a caravan park in North Wales two summers ago.

I try to shake away the memories as I shout, "I'm running in the right direction this time!"

"Yes you are. Go, Storm!" Mum shouts. After we jog round the park a few times, my worries about the money and the house fade away. I have a steady pace and, just like the trees swaying, I'm going at my own rhythm. Everything feels calm. Then I feel my phone ping in my pocket.

Later today, I'm going to the Trafford Centre with Zarrish and Melissa to find outfits for the funfair. It was Melissa's idea and, even though I can't afford anything other than earrings with the money I have left over from my birthday, I still agreed to go because Melissa added me to a WhatsApp group with her and Zarrish last night. Mum has been working extra shifts at the hospital because money is tight with the house repairs, so I definitely can't ask her for money to buy a new outfit. When I told them that, Zarrish said it's okay but Melissa completely ignored me and continued to add photos of outfits onto the group chat she called "Storm's Makeover Inspo". I thought she was joking about the makeover but she's been talking about nothing else for days. The fair is supposed to be fun. It's supposed to be about going on rides that make you scream, eating all the candyfloss that your stomach can take and shouting about the rigged games, when we lose every single time. I'm hoping that when we get to the fair they'll both remember that. I open the group chat.

Zarrish: Can you meet us there?

I frown. I never meet Zarrish anywhere; we always go together. She knows I would never go anywhere by myself.

I begin typing.

Storm: You know I'm not allowed to get the bus to the Trafford Centre by myself. Can you not meet me at the bus stop?

I turn round to see that Mum is quite far behind me. She's still jogging, although it looks like she should probably stop for a break. Even Minnie is panting as she runs next to her. My phone pings with another text from Zarrish.

Zarrish: I stayed at Melissa's last night so the bus stop is too far for us to get to.

I didn't know they were having a sleepover. I feel my stomach knot up. That's the second time that they've done something outside of school without me. I wonder if Melissa saw the text that I sent to Zarrish about not wanting a makeover. I really hope not.

I can see that Melissa is typing.

Melissa: Just don't mention to your mum and

dad that we won't be getting the bus

together. They won't know.

Maybe I should lie to Mum and Dad. I really don't want to be left out again, but the thought of getting the bus on my own is scary. What if someone sits next to me and I have to ask them to move so I can get off when it's my stop? I begin typing before deleting it quickly. I don't know what to do. I begin typing again. I'm going to have to lie.

Storm: I'm not really feeling well. I don't think I can make it anyway.

I can't lie to Mum and Dad, besides there's no point. I don't know how they do it, but they always find out what I'm doing eventually. I also don't want to tell Melissa that I'm not lying to my parents. Not when she's starting to like me enough to add me to a group chat. I don't want her to call me a goody two shoes again. I bet they're just going to be talking about their sleepover and it's going to be awkward listening to them, so maybe it's a good thing that I can't go.

Zarrish: Feel better soon xx

Melissa: Don't worry we can sort your
makeover without you. x

"Who – was – that?" Mum asks, struggling to speak as she stops next to me. She tells me to wait before we start again, so she can get her breath back.

"Oh, it was Zarrish," I say putting my phone away.

"What time are you going out again?" Mum asks.

"We're not going any more," I respond with a shrug.

"That's a shame," Mum says, waving across the park at another friend she has spotted. "But never mind, that means we can practise more. By this rate, I'll be fit enough to run in the championships too." She smiles, putting her arm round me.

We're met with a tower of boxes in the hallway when we get back to Grandma's house. Dad went back home when we were at the park and it looks like he has returned with more of our clothes and belongings. Mum and Dad keep speaking in hushed tones. From what I can gather from their private conversation, the water pipe that needs replacing wasn't insured. This means that we have to stay at Grandma's house for even longer. We were only supposed to be staying for a few days, but looking at the tower of boxes, I get the feeling that we're going to be staying a lot longer than planned. I don't know how much longer I can cope sharing a room with Isaiah. I miss my own room and my own space. Now the only time I can think properly is when I'm running. As Mum and Dad unpack, I leave the house through the front door to escape the chaos. Grandma has the only front garden on the street in full bloom, so when I sit down, I'm hidden in a forest of petunias and irises.

"What you doin'?"

I jump and get tangled in the petunias as Ryan peers his head through Grandma's purple perennials. "You scared me!" I say, pulling myself up. Now that I'm not going out with Zarrish and Melissa, I have nothing to do today, so I decided to start the science homework. I put my hand over my sheet of paper but it's too late. Ryan has already seen what I'm doing.

"Is that Saturn?" he asks. When Ms Morrison said that Ryan and I will be working together on our science homework project, I decided that it would be best if I just did it by myself. Ryan usually waits until he's given a detention before handing his homework in and it's usually delivered crumpled from his blazer pocket. There is absolutely no way that I'm getting in Ms Morrison's bad books.

"We're supposed to do it together!" he says. "Stop drawing and meet me at my grandad's in two minutes," he adds, now running back to his house.

"But—"

Ryan has disappeared before I have time to object to his plan.

I'm surprised that Ryan would want to do anything to do with school on a Saturday, although it might be a good idea, because during the week he's either in a detention or busy getting into trouble that will lead to a detention.

I shout over the boxes piled up in the hallway that I'm going to Ryan's before heading over. He calls me round the back and greets me on his back doorstep, his arms full of cardboard boxes.

"What are they for?" I ask. He drops them on the kitchen floor before disappearing out of the room only to appear a few moments later with PVA glue and paint.

"For our solar system," he says. "I was thinking that we could make a massive solar system, like this big," Ryan says, stretching his arms as wide as he can. For someone who claims to never have his pencil case in lesson, he sure has a lot of art supplies at home.

"I thought we could draw our solar system," I say, holding up my sketch and following him inside. I'm terrible at drawing but I'm even worse at arts and crafts. I'm hopeless at anything that requires cutting, threading or gluing.

"That's boring. Don't worry, me and my grandad build stuff all the time. We've got this."

I watch nervously as Ryan begins ripping up cardboard boxes enthusiastically. I look at my phone as a photo pops up of Zarrish and Melissa posing in a shop mirror with different hats on. Maybe I should've just joined them, even if it meant lying. It's all they're going to be talking about on Monday. Music starts blaring from Ryan's laptop as he hands me foam material to start making Venus. Or is it Neptune? Whatever it is, I put down my sketch and begin covering the material in blue paint.

I look up to see Ryan staring at me.

"What?" I say, shifting in my seat.

"How do you know this song?" he asks, stopping what he's doing.

"What song?" I say knowing full well what song he's talking about.

"The song you're singing along to," he grins.

"I'm not singing," I say. My face feels hot. I didn't even realize that I was singing along to the music. Dad plays this song every time he has a gig; it's his encore song and there's always time for an encore, whether the crowd want one or not.

I turn the question back on Ryan. "What do *you* know about this song?" It's not exactly what people play at school. I definitely won't be hearing it coming out of Melissa's phone when she blasts her music at lunchtime and I know it won't be on her stupid fair playlist.

"Cos it's a tuuuuune," he says, singing it louder.

"Sing it!" he suddenly shouts before turning the volume up.

I look down at whatever it is I'm painting to stop myself from smiling at Ryan, who is belting out *Hey Jude* at the top of his voice.

"Come on, you were just singing it," he shouts, pushing his chair backwards as he stands up.

"No, I wasn't," I say.

He drops his paintbrush and stands on his chair, singing like he is performing to a packed-out crowd at Manchester Arena.

"Having fun?" Ryan's grandad says, walking into the kitchen. Ryan jumps off his chair as his grandad comes in and heads over to the kitchen to put the kettle on.

"Do you want a hot chocolate?" his grandad asks. I've never seen Ryan so helpful before, as I watch him get out three mugs from the cupboard. Ms Morrison and Mrs Osei wouldn't believe their eyes if they could see him now.

Ryan puts my mug of hot chocolate down in front of me.

"Your grandad is nice," I say as his grandad goes back into the living room.

"Yeah, he is," Ryan smiles. I'm curious to know why his smile quickly fades, but I'm unsure of what to say. The hot chocolate is too hot to drink and the paint isn't dry enough to continue working on the planet.

"I love this song," I finally say over the sound of *Don't Stop* by Fleetwood Mac belting out of his laptop. The song reminds me of car rides to summer music festivals to watch my dad's band play.

"It's alright, I guess," he says, smiling cheekily.

"It's a *tune*, don't deny it!" I say.

He smiles and I smile too as we both nod along to the music.

CHAPTER 12

"Isaiah's little sister!"

I turn round to see Princess walking towards me. She must have just come from PE because she's holding an ice pop.

It's Monday and despite just spending period one listening to Mr Adams confusing me as I tried to figure out the area of a parallelogram, I'm excited because it's now time for PE. Mr Harris said that we're focusing on the relay race today.

"Good luck for the qualifier!" she smiles before walking into a classroom. How did she know about the qualifier? Isaiah must have told her. It's coming up in just a few weeks and my mind keeps switching from excitement to nerves to excitement again.

After spending Saturday afternoon working on my homework project with Ryan, I spent the rest of the weekend watching athletics videos on YouTube. There was this one video of Team GB's women's relay team. Relay races look fun because you get to be in a group and yes, I usually hate group activities, but the idea of helping my team cross the finish line in first place does sound exciting. I know Zarrish has hated athletics so far, but when we all work together and cheer each other on, I know she'll like it, especially if we're in a team with other girls in our class.

I carry on walking as confusion sweeps over me. Why is everyone smiling at me? A Year Nine gives me a thumbs up and I smile back nervously, wondering what's going on.

"What've you done?" Ryan asks, catching up with me. He got held back in maths for having his head on the desk for most of the lesson.

"I'm not sure," I say hesitantly. This can't all be from Isaiah. As I open the PE doors, Ryan grabs my arm before I can head down the steps to the girls' changing rooms.

"Storm, look!" he says.

I follow Ryan's hand as he points to the large TV screen that displays the PE fixtures. "Your photo was just up there," he says. "Come on," he says, pulling me closer to the screen.

"What's happening?" Koko asks, coming towards us. Ryan barges past people to make way for us to stand in front of the screen.

"Storm's photo comes up, just watch."

So that's why Princess wished me good luck and why everyone was smiling at me on the way down here. I feel nervous as the screen reads out the football fixtures and the tennis matches, before my heart skips a beat. *Join us in wishing the following students good luck for the upcoming Greater Manchester Schools Athletics Championships Qualifier!* The nerves get the best of me as photos of the athletics team start popping up on the screen.

With the crowd building, I regret not rushing to the changing rooms. I try to look for a way out before it gets to me but Ryan notices and blocks my way. "Wait, it hasn't got to your photo yet," he says.

"There you are!" Koko shouts.

I stop panicking and look up to see my photo taking up the entire screen. I can't help but feel a buzz when I see it appear.

"Do you think you'll win and go to the finals?" Koko asks.

"Course she will, she's Isaiah's little sister. Winning is in her genes," Jayden, Isaiah's friend, says butting into our conversation as he walks past. He holds out his fist towards me and I fist-bump him back reluctantly.

"Nah, she's going to win because she's the fastest, not because of Isaiah. Right, Storm?" Ryan says.

"Right," Koko says, speaking for me. But I'm not too sure. When I step into the changing rooms, I'm unable to shake off Jayden's comments. What if I can't be as good as Isaiah? What if I lose?

"HEY, GUYS." Melissa announces her late arrival as she swings the changing-room doors open with a giant thud. Zarrish follows behind her. Everyone looks up and Melissa strides through, shoving bags off the bench and onto the floor to make way for her to sit down.

"Hurry up, Year Seven, your teacher is waiting outside on the field," Miss Scott says, holding the door open. I finish tying my shoelaces and stand up ready to go.

"We're not going yet," Melissa says, pulling me back down onto the bench. I rub my arm from her tight grip and watch helplessly as everyone else filters out. We're the last ones in the changing room, but this doesn't seem to bother Melissa or Zarrish.

"Are you feeling better?" Zarrish asks. It takes me a moment to remember the lie I told them to get out of going to the Trafford Centre on Saturday.

"Oh yeah. I feel fine now, thanks," I say, forcing a gentle smile.

"Saturday was SO good. You missed out, Storm," Melissa says loudly. Zarrish and Melissa begin laughing at private jokes that I don't know, but I smile when they laugh as a way to join in. I glance down at my watch and see with a jolt that class started five minutes ago.

"Stop stressing, Storm," Zarrish says, noticing me. She knows me too well.

"I'm not," I say leaning back. I have to stop myself from falling backwards on the bench as I try my best to look as unbothered as possible. Melissa gives me a dirty look, noticing my stumble before she gets out her phone.

"Come on, let's take a selfie," Melissa says.

Zarrish shimmies over to her. "Come on, Storm," Zarrish says. I shove myself over in time for Melissa's phone to flash.

"Girls, that's an official warning for time wasting. Come out of the changing rooms now."

Miss Scott is standing by the doors looking unimpressed at what she's seeing.

"We're not ready," Melissa snaps. She stands up and turns her back on Miss Scott, waiting for her to walk away. "Has she gone?" Melissa whispers to me. I'm scared to look over at Miss Scott, but I do and see that she has her hands on her hips waiting. I don't answer her, but Melissa knows this means Miss Scott is still stood waiting. Melissa laughs and Zarrish smirks.

"Right, that's now a bad-behaviour point. Keep going and it'll be a detention," Miss Scott snaps back, growing impatient.

"I thought you would want to practise with you being on the athletics team," Miss Scott adds.

"We're not on the athletics team," Melissa snorts.

"I was talking to Storm," Miss Scott says. Melissa and Zarrish both look at me with raised eyebrows. I bow my head but I can still feel their stares. I guess they didn't see the screen as they walked in.

"Alright, alright, we're coming. *Gosh!*" Melissa says, throwing up her hands in the air. She stands up and I take this as a signal to walk quickly out of the changing rooms. I keep my head down so I don't make eye contact with Miss Scott as I walk out. Before I reach the PE doors I stop, noticing that Melissa and Zarrish aren't behind me.

"Girls, do I have to tell you again?" Miss Scott shouts. It takes me by surprise. Miss Scott never raises her voice.

"We know where the field is, you don't need to escort us," Melissa snaps at Miss Scott. How can she speak to Miss Scott like that? Does she want to get into more trouble and write lines again?

"That's an after-school detention for you," Miss Scott says.

"That's so unfair," Melissa says, slamming the doors open as she finally leaves the changing room.

"We haven't even done anything," Zarrish protests, following behind. Zarrish never speaks back to teachers. Not to their faces anyway. I want to rush out onto the field with the rest of my class. I can't get a detention and face spending an hour with Mr Peterson in the hall after school.

"I can make it an afternoon in the exclusion room if you carry on," Miss Scott threatens as she locks the changing-room doors. Melissa shouts about how much she hates this school as we finally make it out onto the field.

"Storm, there you are!"

I try my best to shake off the past few minutes as Teija runs towards me.

"Do you want to be on our relay team?" she says, with Jasmine and Maya standing by her side.

"Yeah okay, let's go to the end of the field," Melissa says, elbowing me until I take a step back behind her. She walks forward until she realizes that no one is following her.

"We're supposed to get into groups of four, so we only need Storm," Teija explains.

I look at Melissa's face as it turns red like a tomato.

"Well, she's with us, aren't you, Storm?" Melissa hisses, pulling my arm until I'm standing with her.

"You're not even a team, there's only three of you," Maya protests, folding her arms.

"Why don't you be with us, Teija?" Melissa suggests. Teija frowns looking as if that's the worst idea she's ever heard.

"Koko is on their team," Miss Scott says, herding Koko towards us. Koko doesn't look wildly keen on this idea either. Melissa and Zarrish both hold their tongues, knowing that they need her to make a four. "Fine." Teija shrugs, turning round with her group.

"Right, girls, come and sit down with your teams now," Mr Harris shouts over, putting cones down on the grass.

"Today we will be practising the relay," he says. "Relays are usually everyone's favourite lesson because you will be racing as a team. Each of you will run a portion of the race, handing the baton to the next person as they go," he continues. I straighten up and listen as Mr Harris shows us how to use the baton. Neither Zarrish nor Melissa are listening but I continue to, hoping to redeem myself after the trouble in the changing rooms.

As soon as Mr Harris finishes, he tells us to find an empty space to practise and I follow Zarrish and Melissa as they run up to the furthest end of the field. "I'm bored," Melissa says, sitting down and taking out her phone. Zarrish sits down beside her. Koko sits down too, leaving a gap between them. She begins drawing in a sketchbook that she has miraculously pulled from under her jumper. I look around, feeling uneasy that no one in my group is doing what they are supposed to be doing.

"I think that Zarrish should run first?" I suggest, trying to put our team in position. I cough loudly to get everyone's attention but nobody looks up.

"It's very important not to drop the baton," I say, holding it in my hand as I continue anyway. When I was watching races online at the weekend, a few teams dropped the baton. If this happens, the whole team is disqualified from the race.

"The person that is waiting for the baton to be given to them must hold out the palm of their hand like this," I say, showing them the hand position I learned from watching relays. I carry on giving pointers about how to do the perfect baton exchange. The more I go on, the more excited I get. I want to take what I learned and put it into action.

"Relax, Storm, you're low-key being annoying," Melissa says interrupting my flow. "Just chill out, it's not that deep."

I drop the baton and sit down in defeat. Teija and her group are practising by the sixth-form building. I smile as her group cheer each other on. I'm happy that Zarrish and Melissa fought for me to be in their group, especially since I've been feeling left out recently, but as I continue to watch

Teija's group, I can't help but wish I went with them. Teija probably won't ask me to be in her group again.

"We should've got Teija to be on our team," Zarrish says, watching me look over.

"I know, yeah, she would have been a lot better than *her* over there," Melissa says, looking at Koko, who has her nose too deep in her sketchbook to notice that Melissa is talking about her.

"Why does Teija want you on her team anyway?" Melissa asks.

"Because Storm is actually good at running," Koko says, suddenly being able to hear.

"Who's talking to you?" Zarrish snaps. Koko shrugs and continues sketching.

"Since when are you on the athletics team anyway?" Zarrish asks.

"Remember the letter I got for the athletics championships? I've been going to club after school to practise," I explain.

"Oh, I didn't know you actually went," she says.

"I wasn't going to but Isaiah—"

"Urgh can we change the conversation, you guys are boring me," Melissa interrupts.

We all look up at Teija's group screaming as they race another team. "Well done, girls," I can hear Miss Scott cheering along with Teija and her friends as they cross the finish line in first place.

"Is everyone in this school a weirdo?" Melissa says, turning her back on the rest of our class, who are in teams racing against each other. "Why do you look so mad? Go over and join them if you really want to," she sneers at me.

"I don't want to," I mumble, telling a lie. I wish I did go with Teija and her friends. That way I could be putting the techniques I learned in athletics club into practice, all while joining in with my class.

"Then you need to relax, you're irritating me," she adds.

"Yeah, chill out, Storm," Zarrish says to me, to my surprise. I can't believe Zarrish would take Melissa's side. I have finally found something that I'm good at and Zarrish would rather we sit here watching videos on her phone. Remembering my plan to be more like them so I'm not left out, I try to fix my face so that I look unbothered.

"I'm not mad," I lie.

"Good, now listen to this drama that happened yesterday, you won't believe it," Melissa says, sitting up straight as if she's about to tell an epic story. Melissa and Zarrish spend ages gossiping about an argument that happened in the schoolyard with people we don't even know, and I can't do anything but watch the relay races happening around the field, wishing I was taking part. I wish Melissa would go back to her old school so everything can go back to normal. Since when does Zarrish care about silly arguments in the playground? I hate that Zarrish was made to look after her. Melissa is changing everything and, just like a spectator at an athletics race, I can only sit back and watch.

CHAPTER 13

"Get a bongo drum each and form a circle," Mr Johnson says as we head into music after break time. I dodge out of the way of Abdul and Ryan as they play tug of war over the best drum. "They're all the same!" Mr Johnson shouts over as my class battle it out. I manage to grip one that no one seems to want and carry it to the circle formed in the middle of the classroom.

"Feet down and book away," Mr Johnson says sitting down in the circle next to Koko, who is using her drum as a footstool with her nose deep in a graphic novel.

"Now, everyone follow my lead," Mr Johnson says, still watching Koko until she puts her graphic novel in her blazer pocket. He then pats the drum once and we copy. He pats twice, we pat twice. He goes faster, we go faster.

"Okay, I think we all need to practise our rhythm a bit

more," Mr Johnson says, watching in horror as Abdul and his mates bang on the drum to their own terrible tune. "Listen to me, I'm going to bang my drums and I'm going to make a rap to the beat."

He bangs his drums as he raps.

"My name is Mr Johnson, yeah, I like drumming, yeah, but I hate mushrooms, yeah, but I like drumming, yeah."

He stops and pauses. "We are going to go round the circle and you are each going to change the words to your likes and dislikes but keep the beat the same."

I slouch down. I hate activities like this. What am I going to say? There are four people before me. *Think.*

It's Koko's turn first. "My name is Koko, yeah, I like drama, yeah, but I hate dogs, yeah, but I like drama, yeah." The classroom erupts.

"Nah that's snide, how can you hate dogs?" Ryan shouts, putting his head up for the first time.

"I don't like animals," she says.

Asha shakes her head in dismay. "How can you say that?"

Mr Johnson raises his hand to stop the noise. "Everyone has their preferences," he says.

"What does that mean?" Koko asks.

"It means we all have different likes and interests," Miss Scott explains, even though I know she finds it weird that

Koko doesn't like animals. I mean, who dislikes animals?

"Okay, Asha. Go ahead," Mr Johnson says.

Asha begins beating the drum. "My name is Asha, yeah, I like maths, yeah, but I hate pizza, yeah, but I like maths, yeah." The class erupts.

"Wait. A. Second," Koko says, clapping her hands to emphasize each word. It's true that she likes drama. "First of all, how can you like maths?"

Ryan cuts her off. "Who hates pizza?"

Asha folds her arms. "You come and do it then," she says to Ryan. Ryan instantly gets up and moves to a chair in the circle.

"I should've chosen a different topic," Mr Johnson whispers to Miss Scott, who nods in agreement.

Ryan starts beating the drum in a wildly different beat than Mr Johnson's and shouts, "My name is Ryan, yeah, I like Man City, yeah, I hate United, yeah, but I like Man City, yeah."

He stops. For a split second I think there will be silence, but the class erupts.

"United are better!" Abdul shouts.

"Actually, Liverpool are better," Asha shouts, to which the whole class shouts in sync, "LIVERPOOL?"

"I think we should stop," Mr Johnson says, closing the

144

door so nobody outside can hear the chaos within our classroom. For a moment, I feel relief that I won't have to speak, but the rest of my class protest.

"No, we'll be quiet!" Koko whispers loudly.

"This lesson is actually fun, sir," Ryan says.

Mr Johnson laughs nervously. "We haven't got to the lesson part yet, but let's carry on seeing as you're all enjoying it. Storm's turn now," he says, pointing to me. I'm sat frozen to my seat as everyone waits for me to start.

"Go on then," Koko says impatiently.

"What do you like?" Mr Johnson asks. My mind wanders. What should I say? I don't want everyone to laugh at me. Everyone is staring at me now.

"She likes running," Ryan says.

"Okay and what do you hate?" Mr Johnson asks me.

"She hates speaking," Abdul taunts. Laughter fills the circle as I curl up.

"At least when she speaks it's not the trash that comes out of your mouth," Ryan shouts. The class erupts again. I smile at Ryan gratefully for sticking up for me.

"Okay, let's move on to the main part of the lesson," Mr Johnson says, telling us we've let ourselves down by being silly.

"But, sir, we haven't finished yet!" Koko protests.

"I know, but at this rate we will be here all day and we need to get on with the main part of the lesson," he says to my relief.

"Storm, work with Ryan please," Mr Johnson says, ushering us into pairs. I go over to an empty part of the classroom far away enough from Abdul and wait for Ryan, who is on the other side of the room rummaging through the percussion instruments. Every pair has to create an original two-minute musical piece to perform. In this moment, I'd take maths over this nightmare.

"Okay, you take this," Ryan says, handing me an instrument.

"What are they?" I ask, holding the wooden shell shapes tied together with string.

"They're castanets," he replies. "You play them like this," he says, taking one in each hand. He begins to dance round the room, creating a clapping noise with the castanets as he impersonates a flamenco dancer.

"I'm not doing that!" I say half-laughing and half-mortified if Ryan thinks I'm going to copy his dance moves.

"You don't have to. Play it your way," he says, handing me back the castanets.

"Go on, practise. It's only us. Forget about them," he says, watching me scan the room cautiously to see if anyone is looking.

146

He starts playing the drums and I listen to the rhythm before clapping the castanets in my hands. We continue playing, with Ryan writing down the tempo and rhythm of his tune.

"Do you want to perform at the lunchtime showcase?" Mr Johnson says, as he walks over to check how we're doing.

"NO!" Ryan and I shout at the same time.

"But you sound really good," Mr Johnson says, eyes wide with disappointment.

I don't care how good we are, there is no way that I'm getting up in front of the entire school.

"You should do the showcase," I tell Ryan once Mr Johnson has moved on.

"Me? Not a chance!" he says.

"Why not? Are you scared?" I ask, wondering what happened to the Ryan who was standing on a chair singing in his kitchen.

"No!" he protests. "I just have stuff to do," he lies.

"Like what?" I ask.

"You're really good at music," I say, not dropping it. It's true. He's not even had his head on the desk or stomped out of the classroom once. He hasn't had his name written on the board or been given a consequence.

"What can I say? I'm full of surprises," he smiles. I'm beginning to see that.

"Do you really think that I should do the showcase?" he asks. I can see a glimmer of excitement and fear in his eyes.

"Yes!" I say. I'm surprised that Ryan is hesitating. I didn't think he would be scared of anything. He taps the bongo drum with the tip of his fingernails as he thinks about it. "Maybe I should," he says.

"I'll tell sir!" I say, jumping up ready to run to Mr Johnson before he changes his mind.

"Ryan Taylor!"

Ms Morrison strides into the classroom and I sit back down immediately.

"Come with me," she orders. I look towards Ryan, who still has his hands on the bongo drum.

"No," he replies in defiance, sitting back in his chair. Ms Morrison taps her zebra-print stiletto shoe and pinches the bridge of her nose in frustration.

"Ryan, I'm not asking you. I'm telling you. You're spending the rest of the day in the exclusion room for what you did at break time."

What did he do at break time that was so bad he has to leave lesson?

Everyone turns to Ryan to see what he will do next, but he

doesn't do anything. He stays still. "I'm going to start counting and if you are not out of the door by the time I get to five, you're in serious trouble," she warns.

"One, two," Ms Morrison starts counting.

"Ryan, just go!" Koko whispers loudly.

"Just go, man," Abdul shouts, growing impatient.

Ms Morrison's cheeks flare to a strawberry red as she gets to five without any movement from Ryan. "I'm *so* sorry to the rest of the class that Ryan is disrupting the lesson. I'm going to have to ask everyone to stand up and line up outside until he decides to make the right choice," Ms Morrison says. Everyone gives dagger stares and mutters to Ryan as we're forced to leave the classroom. Ryan looks on with a stony face and I get a flashback to when he sat on his garden wall last week waiting for his mum, who didn't turn up. I want to help, to tell him to go with Ms Morrison before it gets any worse, but I can only look at him helplessly as I follow my class out into the corridor.

"Yo, what did he do?" Abdul asks around. I don't want to join in the gossip but I want to know too, so I listen in as everyone chimes in on what happened at break time. Grace says he started a water fight and Mr Adams got drenched trying to get everyone to stop.

Asha whispers that she saw him surrounded by a group

of Year Nine girls by the break shack. "They looked like they were egging him on to start something," she continues, until Mr Johnson hushes everyone to be quiet.

I bite my nails in frustration. I wish Ms Morrison could've seen how great he's been in music. Then maybe she would give him a second chance to stay in lesson. I startle at the sound of a crashing thud coming from inside the classroom. The door flies open and Ryan storms out. Ms Morrison follows behind him, her heels clinking until she turns the corner of the corridor.

"Right, guys, help tidy the room before the bell goes," Mr Johnson says walking into the now trashed classroom. There are chairs and drums thrown in all directions. I pick up the piece of paper that Ryan was writing his music beats on and fold it safely into my blazer pocket before helping to tidy up.

When I get to the dining hall at lunchtime, Zarrish and Melissa are sat down at a table in the middle, both too busy looking at their phones to notice that I've arrived.

"Oh, hey," Zarrish says, finally looking up. She's still giggling from whatever is on her phone. Melissa looks up to see that it's me before looking back at her phone. "Sorry, it's just about something that happened in lesson. You wouldn't get it," she says.

I wait for them to finish looking at their phones but they are taking too long. I'm not in the mood to talk anyway. I hear the sound of music being played outside at the showcase in the courtyard and feel frustrated that Ryan isn't there performing.

"What do you think, Storm?" Zarrish asks, snapping me out of my thoughts.

"Think of what?" I ask.

Zarrish looks frustrated. "About this hairstyle. I sent you the photo last night."

"Gosh, keep up, Storm," Melissa scoffs.

"No, you didn't," I say confused. I scroll through my phone to see no new messages from Zarrish.

"Oh, my bad," says Zarrish. "I just sent it to Melissa by accident, I'll send it to you now."

My phone pings with an image of a girl with blonde highlights. I look back to Zarrish, who is looking at me waiting for me to answer. "So do you think I'll get away with it?" she asks. Of course she won't. Mrs Osei notices everything, but Melissa is adamant that she should do it anyway.

"Hey, Storm, see you tomorrow!" Danielle waves over to me.

"What's happening tomorrow?" Zarrish asks as I wave back to her.

"Tomorrow is the athletics qualifier," I say softly. Melissa and Zarrish both look at each other and I get the feeling that I've missed another conversation. I've been practising all week at athletics club and at home too but after my photo was plastered on the screen in PE for everyone to see, my nerves have taken over again.

"Come on," Melissa orders us up from the table, uninterested in the athletics qualifier.

"Where are we going?" I ask.

"Outside to watch the basketball," she says huffily, like she's already told me this before. "It would be a lot easier if you were in our form. That way we wouldn't have to repeat everything twice," Melissa complains.

"Please take your tray," the dinner lady says, ready to clean the table. Melissa laughs and continues to walk away. "Young lady," the dinner lady shouts at Melissa, who turns and laughs, before running out of the dining-hall door. I pick up Melissa's tray and put it on the tray rack.

"Hurry up, Storm," Zarrish shouts.

"I'm coming," I mutter, running out of the doors to catch them up.

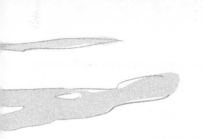

CHAPTER 14

I'm so nervous about the qualifiers that I almost didn't come in to school today. Everybody knows that it's today too, because I came to school in my PE kit. Dad made me a special athlete's breakfast, which was just porridge but it had berries making a shape of a medal. I even got a lift to school, so I didn't have to worry about Isaiah making me late with fashion-show drama.

"Good luck, Storm!" Mrs Osei sings when it's time for me to leave English.

"Yes, you're going to be brilliant!" Miss Scott echoes.

"Break a leg. Not literally, of course," Koko says.

"Thanks," I say nervously, closing the classroom door behind me. I wish everyone didn't know that I was racing today. It's going to make it so much harder if I lose. The student entrance is packed with people waiting to get on the school bus. I didn't think it was going to be this full. When Mr Harris tells us all to get on the bus, I don't see Teija or even Danielle, so I find a seat at the front. Edie, a Year Eight, who I remember from athletics club, almost takes me out with a sign that says, "GO DAISY MILL!" in bold, gold, glittery letters. As the chatter from behind me fills the bus, I take out the event schedule and begin reading it so I don't look completely tragic sitting by myself. I must've read the event schedule a thousand times since Mr Harris handed them out during last athletics club. Fifteen schools from across Greater Manchester are taking part. The most important thing I need to remember is that only the top three from each race qualify for the finals, so I have to make sure I finish at least third. I put the event schedule back in my bag and scroll through my phone to see if I have any text messages. I have one from Mum and Dad and another from Isaiah. I was expecting a good luck message from Zarrish but I've not heard from her. I wonder if she forgot that I'm racing today.

I'm the first to get off when we arrive at Longford Park. The sight of a proper athletics track turns my legs to jelly. I wasn't expecting the track to be this big. The sight of other schools already warming up with their numbers pinned to their T-shirts sends a shiver down my spine. We follow Mr Harris to our designated area in the stand where the Year

Eights tie their banners to the front railings that separate the seated area from the track. I have no idea where to sit until Teija puts her bag next to mine.

"Okay, I'm actually scared now," she says, sitting next to me. I didn't think Teija would be scared but I'm glad she said that, because I'm terrified.

"What are you racing?" she asks.

"Two hundred metres and four hundred metres," I reply. "What about you?" I add, hoping that I don't have to run against her.

"I'm running the eight hundred metres," she says. *Phew.* That's one less thing to worry about.

Danielle calls us over to join in with a warm-up before the Year Tens are called up first. I wish her good luck before running back to the stands to watch the first race of the day.

"Why are you nervous? It's not your race." Teija nudges me, noticing my legs trembling. Danielle has one chance to qualify and she has do to so in front of a stand crammed full of spectators watching on. I can't help but feel nervous for her.

"Go, Danielle!" Razan cheers, her voice echoing around the stands until everyone follows her chant, "Daisy Mill! Daisy Mill!" Other schools begin cheering too until a steward holding a bell near the starting line waves for everyone to stop. Razan smiles broadly, impressed by her own ability to start a chant before the stand is hushed into silence.

"On your marks. Get set. GO."

The stands erupt back into chants as the Year Tens leap off the starting line. Danielle takes off well but people sprint past her and she starts to fall behind. "Come on, Danielle!" Razan shouts. Everyone is standing up now. I follow Teija down to the railings not believing what I'm seeing.

"Go, Danielle!" Razan shouts louder. Danielle picks up pace and inches closer to the person in front. How is she not winning? She's running fast like she does in athletics club, but everyone else is fast too and when she crosses the finish line, she's in fourth place. She's not made it to the finals.

"Well, there's no hope for the rest of us," Rico sighs gloomily as we all sit back down.

"Don't say that, we've got this!" Razan says. She's trying to be positive but I can hear the doubt in her voice. Danielle is the fastest person in our entire school and she just lost.

"Unlucky, Danielle," Razan says gently, patting her on the back as she makes her way back to our area. She sits down looking teary-eyed as everyone continues to console her. Watching Danielle has made me feel more nervous. If Danielle lost, what chance do I have?

* * *

"Storm, you're up next," Mr Harris says. It's the last few events of the day and it's finally my turn to race.

"You've got this!" Razan says, getting herself ready to take charge of our school chants again. That's easy for her to say. She won both her qualifying events. Edie did too, and so did Rico and Teija. It's just me to go.

The starting line feels like a million miles away. I walk over, trying my best to remember what Mr Harris said to me in athletics club. *Keep my head straight and shoulders down. Don't look left. Don't look right. Focus on my own lane.*

I try to breathe through the queasiness I'm feeling but the chants echoing from the stands are not helping. Mr Harris never mentioned that there would be so many people here. The finish line is right in front of the stands, which means everyone is going to have the perfect view of me losing.

The cheers from the stands come to an abrupt end. I put my hand on my chest, wondering if anyone can hear my heart thumping as loud as I can. I follow the girls I'm running against and get myself into position on the white line. I wish I had a way out of this. *Why did Isaiah hand in my consent form?* I should've gone along with Zarrish and forgot about athletics. *What have I done?*

"On your marks. Get set. GO."

I'm left on the starting line as people dart past me.

Startled, I stumble off the line, trying my best to catch up with everybody already speeding down the track. I turn to look to the Daisy Mill area in the stands. Everyone is screaming but I can't make out what they're saying. Teija looks worried. Does she think I'm going to lose?

"Keep going, Storm!" Mr Harris bellows from the sidelines. *Don't look left, don't look right.* I remember his words from athletics club and will myself on. Overtaking the person in front of me gives me confidence to keep sprinting. With my feet pounding the track, I make ground and continue to storm past several of my competitors. I'm in the flow with my nerves easing with every step. I take one final stride to push myself over the finish line. I have no idea where I came.

"Good race." A girl dressed head to toe in red reaches for my hand to shake. I spot the logo on her PE kit; she's from St Margaret's. From the smile on her face I know she came first.

"Congratulations," I say, trying my best to be happy for her even though she just beat me. I tried really hard to catch up, but it looks like I was too late.

"I guess I'll see you at the finals," she says.

I look at her, bewildered. "What?" I reply. She doesn't have time to answer me as she gets pounced on by her teammates all cheering her name. I look towards the Daisy Mill area where Rico and Teija are jumping up and down in excitement as Razan and Edie whoop with joy. A steward wearing a yellow high-vis hands me a ticket that tells me where I've finished in the race. I take it, my hands shaking.

Number three.

I did it. I'm going to the finals.

"Come to the back," Teija says, holding up the bus until I have unfastened my seat belt and followed her down the aisle. Both of my qualifying medals jingle from side to side as I walk. "Keep going all the way," Teija says.

"Isn't the back for Year Tens and Elevens?" I whisper.

"Don't worry about them," she insists.

"Hi, guys," Edie says, waving for us to sit with her and Razan. Teija lets me have the window seat as we sit adjacent to them.

"Sir, can you put some music on?" Razan shouts as we pull out of the car park. I turn to look back at the athletics track, where I finished in the top three for both my two-hundred-metre and four-hundred-metre races to qualify for the Greater Manchester Schools Athletics Championships. I can't get over it.

"Okay, I'll put the radio on," Mr Harris says as the bus pulls out.

"No, sir, from my phone," Razan says, passing her phone along the bus to Mr Harris.

"Wait, I haven't watched the videos yet," Edie says, grabbing Razan's phone back.

"Oh yeah, I forgot that I recorded everyone's races," Razan says, clapping her hands together to grab everyone's attention.

"It's Storm's race first," she says with everyone now glued to her phone.

"I'm not going to lie, I was worried for you," Rico says, turning to look at me with my race now playing out. I smile along anxiously with the giggles that seem to be spreading around the back of the bus in agreement. Turns out, no one expected me to win after I stumbled at the start of my first race.

"You kept looking into the stands!" Rico continues to analyse my race. He's right but I couldn't help it. The more I saw everyone watching, the more worked up I got.

"Look! You can hear me screaming at you to move," Razan shouts, making my relive the part of my race I wish I could forget.

"You're quiet, aren't you?" Razan says, giving her phone to Rico so he can watch his race. I shrug, not knowing how to answer. I should know what to say by now because everyone always tells me this.

"Leave her, not everyone is obnoxiously loud like you," Edie says. Razan hits her friend jokily.

"It was just an observation," she says. "You're quiet; I'm loud...Edie is weird." Edie hits Razan in response but she's laughing now.

"And Teija is..." She stops to think about it. "I don't even know what you are, you're hard to read." Teija raises her eyebrow and shakes her head laughing. "Anyway, what I'm saying is, life would be boring if we were all the same. So if someone calls you quiet then don't take it as an insult. Take it as a compliment," Razan concludes, trying to recline her seat back. "That's what I do when people say that I'm loud – like last week when Ms Morrison told me that I was too loud to join science club."

"You should've seen Ms Morrison's face when Razan kept saying thank you, as if being told you're disruptive is a compliment," Edie adds, grinning as she turns to Razan. "She took great pleasure in escorting you out."

"She actually said you're too loud?" Teija asks.

"Well, not exactly, but she did pull a face when I walked in and then continued to tell me to lower my voice for the next fifteen minutes before sending me out. Their loss."

I laugh as I picture it. Ms Morrison doesn't have much patience. She doesn't strike me as the kind of teacher who willingly gives up her free time for students.

"So why do you come to athletics club?" I ask.

"I actually like athletics," she says. "Plus, ice pops," she smiles.

"Now we've all made it to the finals, we need something that makes us feel like a proper team," Rico says from several seats forward. "Anyone got any ideas?" he asks everyone.

I think about it. "We should get hoodies," I say to Teija quietly.

"Hoodies?" she says.

"My mum is in a roller-skating club and they all have matching hoodies," I explain.

"Your mum is in a roller-skating club?" she asks, eyebrows raised.

"Yeah," I say nervously.

"That's cool," she says. "You should tell them your idea," Teija says.

I look around the bus. I can't just shout it out. "No, you can," I say.

"What about matching hoodies?" Teija shouts. The bus goes silent. I knew they would think it was a bad idea.

"Teija, that's genius!" Razan grins.

"Yes, Teija!"

The whole bus is now talking and debating what kind of

hoodies to get. Mr Harris likes the idea too. I guess it wasn't a bad idea after all. I slouch in my seat, secretly disappointed that nobody knows that it was my idea.

It's already lunchtime by the time our bus arrives back at school. I rush to the dining hall hoping to find Zarrish. I'm desperate to fill her in on what happened.

"Hey," Zarrish says as I walk over to the table where she is sat with Melissa. She's got her arm around Melissa, who has her head bowed as if she has been crying.

"What happened?" I ask, not knowing if I really want to find out.

"Melissa has to go to the exclusion room," Zarrish says.

"What for?" I say. Getting sent to the exclusion room is even worse than detention; it's only for people who are in serious trouble. I've only ever seen Ryan sent there. Melissa pulls her blonde hair from her face but there are no tears, only an angry expression that makes me feel uncomfortable, like it's aimed at me.

"That stupid dinner lady complained about me to Mrs Osei. She had the cheek to say that I was rude because I didn't take my tray. That's her job! I'm texting my mum. They must be mad if they think I'm going in exclusion."

Melissa types so hard that I wouldn't be surprised if her thumbs went through her phone.

"Why are you in your PE kit?" Zarrish asks, noticing for the first time.

"It was the athletics qualifier today," I say reluctantly, now that they are both giving me daggers stares for looking so happy.

Zarrish thinks for a moment, trying to remember what I'm talking about.

"Hey, Storm, I heard you got through to the finals," Ryan calls, walking over to our table. He sits down next to me. "Did you get a medal?" he asks. I pull out both my medals from my jumper. I look at Zarrish with a small tang of pride, but she glances at my medals for a moment before looking away without a single reaction. I try my hardest to hide my disappointment that she didn't congratulate me, but it's really hard. She's supposed to be my best friend.

"Nice one," Ryan smiles.

I haven't seen Ryan since our music lesson. He spent all yesterday afternoon and this morning in the exclusion room for the incident that caused Ms Morrison to come looking for him. He protested that it wasn't him who started the water fight, but that doesn't matter. Ryan is always there when something kicks off, so he usually gets the blame. She also added an extra punishment on top of this too because he refused to follow her instructions and trashed the classroom. He's now on the yellow report that he's been threatened with all year, so he *has* to be good or he's going to be excluded.

"Ew, go away, nobody wants you here," Melissa snaps.

"It's the first time we've qualified in ages. Mr Harris is with Mrs Osei now; all the teachers are talking about it," he continues, ignoring Melissa.

"We?" Zarrish says.

Ryan huffs. "We as in Daisy Mill Academy," he explains. "I bet you're buzzin', Storm. It's a big deal apparently."

Melissa slams her phone down at a text she just read. I guess her mum isn't going to get her out of her punishment.

"Can you all just shut up! Like anyone cares about stupid athletics. Besides, Teija and her mates just walked past and from what I overheard *you* came third. It's not like you won or anything," Melissa snaps.

"Shut up! Third is still good, isn't it, Zarrish?" Ryan jumps to my defence.

Everyone turns to look towards Zarrish for her reaction but she keeps her head down, using her fork to fiddle with the contents of her plate.

"Didn't I tell you to do one?" Melissa jeers at Ryan.

"Nobody wants you here. Not even your mum wants you, that's why you live with your grandad."

My hands don't reach my mouth fast enough to cover my gasp. Ryan slams the table with clenched fists then picks up a cup of water, but before he can throw it in Melissa's direction Mr Peterson grabs it from behind.

"Ryan Taylor, out now!" he shouts. Melissa's rage fades as she turns to taunting Ryan. He has to be held back as she laughs and waves at him being escorted out of the dining hall.

How did she even know about Ryan living with his grandad? I turn to Zarrish and as our eyes meet she looks away quickly. She must have told Melissa what I said about Ryan waiting for his mum. I didn't mean it in a bad way, not in the way that Melissa just made it out to be. I try to find the words to tell Melissa that she was out of order but they catch in my throat as she glares at me.

CHAPTER 15

"Here comes the superstar!"

I finally turn down Grandma's street – Isaiah had me waiting for half an hour after school so he could sign more teachers up for the fashion show. Mum's friend Julie zooms down the middle of the road towards us. Isaiah reaches out just in time to catch her before she falls into Grandma's marigolds.

"Congratulations, Storm!" Tricia says, skating over too. Mum glides over and joins her friends in sitting on Grandma's garden wall.

"Let's have a look at your medals then." Mum beams.

"What've you got them hidden for?" Tricia asks, as I lift them from under my school jumper. "If it were me, I'd be showing them to anybody who walked past," she adds.

"You must be dead chuffed. It's not every day you qualify

for the athletics championships," Julie says, taking my medals for a closer look.

"Storm Williams, fastest girl in all of Manchester!" Tricia shouts, holding my medals up so they glisten against the sun.

"Hardly," I wince. "I only came third," I say mimicking Melissa's comment. I wonder if everyone else is thinking the same thing.

"Don't say it like that! You did amazing," Julie says as Mum pulls me in for a hug.

I release myself from Mum's hug and take out my phone to show them my four-hundred-metre race where I stumbled. I asked Razan to send me the video so when I'm ready I can use it to practise for the finals.

I watch their reactions as I stumble before their faces light up at me storming down the track.

"Go on, girl!" Tricia shouts watching me cross the finish line.

"Don't fret about the beginning of your race. It's obvious that you're super talented. When you did get going, you sped down the track like lightning," Julie says, shrugging off my stumble as no big deal.

"Can anyone come and watch the final?" Tricia interrupts. She looks at Julie as if they're thinking the same thing.

"We're not anyone, are we? We're practically family! We should definitely be there," Tricia says.

"Oh yes! We can make a huge banner that says 'Go Storm, Go!' in big letters," Mum says.

"We can lead a chant!" Julie says excitedly.

It's hard to tell if they are joking or not. I think they're being serious.

"Two, four, six, eight, who do we appreciate? STORM!"

Tricia and Mum burst out laughing but I'm not seeing the funny side. "Don't worry, we'll work on the chants," Julie says.

"You'll have to tell us where it is so we can get front-row seats," Tricia grins.

This is getting out of hand.

"It's only for competitors, no spectators allowed," I say, interrupting their excitement. I'm not sure this is true but there's absolutely no way that they can come. Today's crowd was bad enough. I almost didn't qualify because I was too worried about everyone watching. I know I would totally freak out if Mum's roller-skating club rocked up with their huge banners and chants too.

"That's a shame." Tricia frowns.

"Yes, it is. I'm sure you can double-check, can't you, Storm?" Mum says, disappointed.

"Yes, course, I'll check," I say, feeling slightly bad about lying but relieved that they won't be coming.

"Hey, seriously though," Mum says, noticing my deflation. "Finishing in the top three with all those other schools competing is something to be proud of."

Maybe she's right. I look down at my medals and allow myself to feel happy. I managed to get this far. I should be proud of myself, no matter what Melissa says. I make a promise to enjoy this moment. I begin to follow Mum inside to celebrate when a car door slamming makes us all turn our heads to the other side of the street. "Someone's in trouble," Julie chuckles. Ryan didn't come back to class after he got escorted away at lunchtime. He steps out of the car and pushes ahead of his grandad, who is shaking his head.

This is all my fault. If I hadn't let slip to Zarrish that Ryan lives with his grandad, then Melissa wouldn't have known.

"Come on, superstar, it's family night," Mum says, saying goodbye to her roller-skating club.

It's Isaiah's turn to choose family night and even though he grumbled about it at first, he ended up choosing the Trafford Centre arcade.

* * *

"Storm, come on the dance machine with me," Mum says, tugging my arm as we walk into the bustling lights of the arcade.

"No way!" I shout over the sound of the dodgems whizzing round behind us. The arcade is crammed with people huddled round each game, long trails of machine tickets behind them. There is absolutely no way she is getting me on the dance machine.

"I'll go on," Dad says.

"You?" we all say in chorus.

"What? Scared I'll show you up with my popping dance moves?" Dad says, wiggling his hips.

Dad doesn't know what he's just started. Nobody challenges Mum to a dance competition and comes out victorious. Me and Isaiah look at each other as both Mum and Dad get ready to compete. "I should add this move to my gig set. What do you think, kids?" Dad says as he jumps up and spins round. I would tell both Mum and Dad to stop, but this is the most fun I've seen them having in ages. In between their extra shifts at work, all they've been doing is dealing with long phone calls and paperwork about the house, so I try to ignore the people watching and laughing around us.

"Come on, Storm, let's go to the basketball game," Isaiah says, ushering me away from Mum and Dad's dance battle.

Isaiah puts a pound in the machine and the basketballs are released. I take the basketball in my hand and shoot. I miss.

"What's up with you then?" he asks. "You should be celebrating your win, but you've been looking dead depressed all day."

I look up at him glumly. "Nothing," I mumble. Isaiah raises his eyebrows.

"Someone got into trouble and it was my fault." I sigh.

"How?" he asks continuing to shoot hoops.

"Well...I told someone something secret and they told someone else and now, even though it's nothing to be ashamed of, they're using it against the person whose secret it is."

Isaiah stops shooting hoops to face me, looking confused. I sigh again.

"I let slip to Zarrish about Ryan living with his grandad and now Melissa is using it against him. She was really nasty to him at lunch and he got so angry. Now he's in trouble and it's all my fault."

Isaiah shoots another hoop. "Just say you're sorry."

"Come on, Diane, let's show them what we've got," I hear Dad shout. We both turn to look at the crowd now forming round Mum and Dad on the dance machine. Mum is twirling around as Dad pretends to play air guitar and the crowd are lapping it up.

"Listen, if Ryan is your mate then he'll know that you didn't mean it in a bad way. Like I said, just apologize and leave it at that. I'm sure he'll forgive you if you're honest with him. Now, can you chill out so I can beat you properly?" he smiles.

I pick up the basketball. "I'm the sports superstar in this family, remember?" I say, aiming a ball at the basket and hearing it whoosh through.

I think about what Isaiah is saying. If I say sorry then I'll have to admit to Ryan that I was talking about him behind his back. I haven't spoken to Zarrish about it either. I want to know why she told Melissa in the first place, but at the same time I don't want her to fall out with me. Speaking up isn't going to be as easy as Isaiah says, but I get the feeling that staying silent isn't going to be easy either.

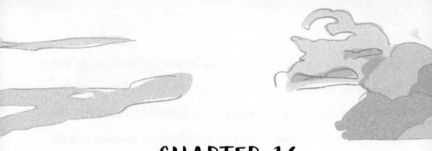

CHAPTER 16

"Storm! They're gonna read your name out in house assembly." It's the next day and Ryan is sat on a small table outside Pankhurst House office. I thought about what Isaiah said all evening and decided to apologize to Ryan as soon as I saw him. Isaiah said that he'll understand that I wasn't trying to be mean or get him into trouble. I just hope he's right.

"How do you know?" I ask, my legs starting to tremble at the thought of going up in front of all of those people. He stops colouring his picture of Air Jordans to look at me.

"I heard Mrs Osei talking before. You're Star of the Week for qualifying for the championships. Mrs Osei thinks you're our secret weapon to beat Turing House on Sports Day. She's proper buzzin' and won't stop talking about it," he says. Surely, if this was true, Isaiah would've told me. But then again, he'd probably know that I'd be worrying about it. "I'm stuck here all day for yesterday, which is stupid 'cos I didn't even manage to throw water over Melissa." Ryan scowls. "I really wish I could've chucked that water on her, she so deserved it, but Mrs Osei said that I was lucky Mr Peterson stopped me doing anything stupid. She gave me this colouring book to do while she's in assembly." He sighs, holding up a book called *Mindful Colouring.*

Realizing that Mrs Osei could come out at any minute – meaning that I'll definitely have to go to assembly – I hurriedly say bye to Ryan and run to the girls' toilets. There is absolutely no way that I can go to assembly. I can't stand up in front of everyone. That's *way* too many people. My breathing quickens and my vision goes blurry as tears fill my eyes. The bell rings and I hear people jostling down the corridors and filing into assembly. I try to take deep breaths and move forward to steady myself on the sink, but my feet feel like they're rooted to the floor. I can't move, so I just stand there and wait for the storm to pass, tears falling onto my shirt.

"You missed it," Koko says as she sits down and shoves felt tips out of the way on the table. Once my legs had stopped shaking enough for me to leave the toilets, I made it to maths before everyone got out of assembly.

"Innit, Asha," she says as Asha comes in to maths. "Mrs Osei awarded you Star of the Week." I try to act surprised and not at all like I just spent the entire time hiding in the girls' toilet.

"You need to go to Pankhurst House office to get your prize," Asha explains.

Koko almost chokes on her water as she remembers this part. "Mr Adams, can I go take Storm to get her prize?" she asks waving her hand in the air. Mr Adams looks at his watch.

"It's a bit late now. You can go at break time. Storm, why weren't you in assembly?"

I try to think of a reason. "I was late to school," I mutter.

"Well, actually, you can go and collect your prize now because I need someone to give this worksheet to Ryan," he says, rummaging in the class book box.

Koko stands up.

"Just Storm, please," Mr Adams says. Koko tuts and sits back down. She's banned from doing jobs for most of our teachers now because she takes too long. Last time Mr Adams asked her to do a job, she took a detour through the sensory garden and didn't come back until ten minutes before the end of the lesson.

I take the work from Mr Adams and head out of the classroom. "Hurry back because we're doing an assessment today," Mr Adams says.

When I arrive at Pankhurst House office, Ryan is inside. I peer through the windows and see both Ryan and Melissa getting a stern talking to from Mrs Osei, who catches me by the window. "There she is! Star of the Week." She beams, opening the office door.

"It's so good to have another Williams in Pankhurst House!" Her bright yellow jumpsuit matches the colour of her nails. She turns down the volume on her walkie-talkie as Mr Peterson's voice echoes out asking for help with a bunch of Year Nines messing about by the fountain. A few copies of Macbeth fall over as she picks up the reward box from her desk. I pick them up and put them back alongside the maths worksheet I brought here for Ryan. "Now, I know you weren't in assembly," Mrs Osei says.

"She was late to school," Ryan says swinging side to side on his chair. I turn to look at him, surprised, because he knows that I wasn't late at all.

"It's fine. I know you're going through a hard time at home at the moment. Don't worry," she says. I look down at the floor hoping not to make eye contact with her. I hate lying but I seem to be doing a lot of it recently.

"But congratulations on qualifying for the athletics championships." Mrs Osei smiles warmly at me. "As you know, our Star of the Week gets to choose a prize from the reward box." She shakes the box around and places it in front of me. The Pankhurst reward box is designed as a treasure chest. You're not allowed to look inside as you take a prize. I put my hand in and move it round the box. I can guess one thing is a book, one is a notebook, a pencil, and something else I can't quite figure out. I pull out a box of Maltesers.

"I have no doubt that you will absolutely smash the finals. Now, Storm, I don't see your name down on the Sports Day list. I expect you'll be signing up for the key events," she says.

"Told you," Ryan says. Mrs Osei raises her hand for Ryan to stop talking. I never thought that I would want to join in on Sports Day, but after Talia mentioned it, I haven't stopped thinking about it.

"We can't waste all of that talent, can we?" She smiles, one eyebrow raised in anticipation.

"Okay," I agree nervously.

"Excellent, excellent," Mrs Osei says, clapping her hands. She reaches behind her desk and pulls out a clipboard. "Here you are," she says, eagerly handing me the signing-up sheet and her purple weighted pen to use. I write my name on two events before handing it back to Mrs Osei, who I still can't make eye contact with, in case she senses my guilt and realizes that I spent assembly hiding in the toilets. She looks at what I've signed up for before also signing me up for the relay and the long jump.

"See, Melissa, you should take a leaf out of Storm's book by being an asset to the school, instead of being rude to members of staff, saying unkind things to your peers, not following the school uniform rules and not taking lessons seriously," she says.

I look towards Melissa, who has her head down, looking at her shoes. Mrs Osei has already stripped her of her hoody, trainers and fake eyelashes, which I'm surprised she got away with wearing for so long. I glance over at the wall covered in thank you cards for Mrs Osei. One card reads, *Mrs Osei Is The G*. I don't think that Melissa would agree right now. Mrs Osei must know that Melissa started the incident yesterday. That's probably why Ryan hasn't been sent to the exclusion room.

"What about me?" Ryan says cheekily. We all turn to look at him.

"Ryan Taylor, I'll get to you in a minute," she says, raising her eyebrows at him. "Okay, Storm, off you go to lesson. I'll email Mr Adams and say that I kept you." She turns to Melissa. "And you can follow me to the exclusion room."

I feel Melissa glaring at me when I walk out of the office. I should be happy that I just signed up for Sports Day but I immediately want to change my mind. I'm clearly in Melissa's bad books, which means Zarrish is going to be in a mood with me too. I leave the office wishing I never came in.

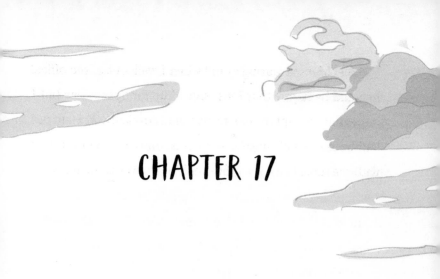

CHAPTER 17

"We need to think of nicknames."

I'm sat in the dining hall by the windows with Edie, Razan and Teija. After-school athletics club has just finished and everyone is waiting to be picked up. Isaiah's band practice finished ten minutes ago but, as usual, he's nowhere to be seen.

Mr Harris surprised us today by telling us that Mr Peterson loved the hoody idea and he is ordering hoodies for everyone on the athletics team. Razan suggested that we should all have nicknames printed on the front. Hopefully we can get them in time for the finals, which are in three weeks. It's getting so close now but I'm trying not to think about it.

We all go silent as we finish off the ice pops Mr Harris gave us.

"My nickname is going to be Queen Bee, obviously," Razan says, writing her nickname on the top of her sheet of paper.

"The only person who calls you that is yourself," Edie laughs, looking out of the window for her mum's car.

Razan grins. "Well, what's your nickname?"

"Excellent Edie," Edie says, putting her hands on her face like she is posing for a photo. Edie and Razan are so different that I'm surprised they are best friends, but they don't seem to mind not liking the same things at all. "Teija should be called Terrific Teija or something," Edie suggests, nudging Razan to write her ideas down.

"Terrific Teija?" Teija squirms.

"You could shorten it to TT! That's so cute," Razan says clapping her hands.

"I don't want to be cute," Teija says cringing.

"What about Storm?" Edie says. Everyone turns to look at me. I've never had a nickname before. I've always just been Storm. Mum and Grandma sometimes call me Stormy, but I don't share this because I absolutely hate it.

"Oh, my mum is here," Edie says jumping up.

"Let's start a group chat, we'll continue discussing nicknames on there," Razan says, handing me her phone. I type in my number and she adds me and Teija before following Edie out of the student entrance.

Mr Harris also informed us that he's put us all down to run in a relay race. My relay team includes me, Razan, Edie and Teija. I couldn't stop smiling when Mr Harris announced the teams because I always have fun when we're together. We're going to be the best relay team in Manchester. That's what Edie says anyway.

It's only me and Teija left in the dining hall now. Teija is waiting for her big sister, Ruby. I guess I'm not the only one that has to wait around for their older sibling. The sound of after-school detention finishing echoes down the corridor and into the dining hall.

"Hi, guys." I turn round and see Melissa standing across the hall. She's been in the exclusion room all day, so I didn't have the chance to find out whether she was mad at me for what Mrs Osei said earlier. I keep telling myself that I'm overthinking it. Melissa has probably moved on to the next drama. Plus, she always says that she doesn't care what Mrs Osei says, so I should stop worrying about it and just chill. Everything is fine. She must not be angry at me because she walks over to our table and sits down.

"I've just spent the entire day in the exclusion room, but at least I didn't have English with stupid Mrs Francis," Melissa says, ignoring me and looking at Teija with a grin.

Teija continues to scroll on her phone before answering. "She's actually alright, you know," Teija says. I don't know who Mrs Francis is but I do know that it doesn't matter how nice she is, Melissa would hate her simply because she's a teacher.

"Yeah, she's alright. Better than the rest of them," Melissa says. I try not to let my jaw drop. That's the nicest thing I have heard her say about a teacher and I know it's only because Teija said it first.

"Z, over here."

I'm surprised to see Zarrish walking towards us, not only because lessons finished ages ago, but also because she absolutely hates being called Z. As she gets closer, I see that her face is puffy and she looks like she's been crying. She sits down a few seats away from us. I know she is really upset because she doesn't like being crowded when she is, she likes her space.

"Is your mum still talking to Mrs Osei?" Melissa asks. Zarrish nods as she flicks the bobble on her wrist up and down. "I can't believe Mrs Osei called your mum into school because you got one detention. We should change houses, I hate her," Melissa adds with a scowl.

I wait for Teija to defend Mrs Osei but she's too busy messaging her sister. I take a gulp. "Mrs Osei is alright you know," I say, trying to reassure Zarrish. Mrs Osei is strict but she's nice too.

"You would say that," Melissa snaps. "You should've heard Mrs Osei in the house office this morning," she says to

Zarrish. "*Storm is such an asset to the school.*" She does her best Mrs Osei impression. "It was so cringe, I was embarrassed for you," she adds, looking at me and laughing. Okay, so maybe she is mad about it. I thought she didn't care about what Mrs Osei says.

She turns to Zarrish, who still isn't smiling. "Why are you so upset? It's only a late detention. See what I have to put up with?" She turns to Teija.

Ruby calls Teija from the other side of the dining hall and Teija stands up. "Later, Storm." She smiles. I watch her walk out of the dining hall with her big sister. I wish Isaiah would hurry up.

"Bye, Teija." Melissa smiles, watching her leave.

"What did Mrs Osei say?" I ask, turning back to Zarrish. I wonder what she could have done for her mum to be called in. Like being sent to the exclusion room, that only happens when you're in serious trouble.

"Mrs Osei said that she's concerned about my behaviour and that I'll be going on house report if I don't improve. I'm going to be in so much trouble when I get home; I might not be allowed to go to the fair," Zarrish groans, putting her head down on the table.

"You better be, I've got my outfit ready," Melissa snaps. I glance at her quickly then look away when she gives me a smirk. What with the qualifiers and athletics club, I'd almost forgotten about the fair and my makeover. Almost.

"What's that?" Zarrish says, brushing her long silky hair out of her face as she looks up from the table. She's pointing at my athletics finals letter. Mr Harris gave them out today in club and I'm so excited, because Mr Harris has agreed to us starting a relay team. I crumple it up to make it look smaller. I don't want to rub it in Zarrish's face that I have a chance to become an athletics champion when she's feeling down.

"Oh this?" I hesitate. Melissa snatches it out of my hand before I have the chance to explain.

"Dear Parents and/or Carers of Storm Williams," she reads with a nasty look on her face.

"Storm Williams has qualified for the Greater Manchester Schools Athletics Championships that will be taking place on 10th May at Manchester Regional Arena. She will be competing in two individual events as well as the relay race. By competing in her events, Storm has the opportunity to help Daisy Mill win the overall championships. We are incredibly proud of Storm's athletics journey this far and want to congratulate her on being a dedicated and hard-working part of the team. She is an asset to the school and we will all be cheering her on.

Yours sincerely,

Mr Harris."

"They say that to everyone," I mutter, taking the letter back from Melissa. I quickly shove it in my blazer pocket.

"Congratulations," Zarrish says coldly.

"Don't stress, Z, we can't all be perfect like Storm."

I feel my cheeks burn up. "I'm not perfect," I say, confused. We sit in silence for a while. Melissa is on her phone and Zarrish is sulking. I don't know what to say or do to make her feel better.

"There you are," Talia says, walking to our table, her signature hoops swinging in her ears. Princess follows behind holding Mrs Osei's iPad. I look at Melissa and Zarrish, wondering who Talia is talking to. "Congrats on qualifying for the championships. I need to take a photo of you for Pankhurst House newsletter," she says looking at me. "Where's your friend gone?" she asks, looking around for Teija before giving up and ushering me to stand next to the Bistro wall.

"Okay, put on your best *We are going to beat Turing House on Sports Day* face," she says, taking several pictures of me with the iPad.

I have no idea how to pose. "Look up, Storm," Princess instructs, "and stand like this," she says, posing to one side with her hands in the air. Her pose makes me laugh, until I see Melissa and Zarrish glaring in my direction. I can't pose the way Princess is telling me to, so I do my best, hoping Talia finishes soon. She shows me the photos, but Zarrish and Melissa are still watching me so I just tell her they're fine.

"I can't believe you're going to be in the house newsletter," Zarrish says, watching Talia and Princess walk away.

"I can't believe she called Teija your friend," Melissa sneers. She tells me that she's only joking, but her face tells me a different story.

"Excellent session today, Storm," Mr Harris shouts across the dining hall. He gives me a thumbs up and I put my thumbs up back at him, until Zarrish gives me a weird look before raising her eyebrows at Melissa.

I want to ask Zarrish why she is being so off with me, but I can't find the words. I have never been more relieved to see Isaiah walking down the corridor. "Isaiah is here, see you tomorrow," I say, giving up on trying to make Zarrish feel better.

"Bye," Zarrish says bitterly.

Isaiah is smiling broadly as I meet him by the student entrance. "What great achievement have you done now?" I ask.

He frowns. "Not me, little sis, you!" He turns his phone screen towards me. A photo of me at the athletics qualifying event is on the school's social page.

I gasp happily and look towards Zarrish, but I stop short of running over to tell her.

"What's up with her?" Isaiah says, looking over too.

I shrug.

That's a good question because, honestly, I have no idea.

CHAPTER 18

"Isaiah, we're going to be late."

As usual, I'm standing by the front door waiting for Isaiah to hurry up so we can get to school before the morning bell.

Ryan rides past on his bike and stops outside Grandma's front gate. "Hi, Storm." I feel guilt sweep over me as soon as I see him. Ryan was with Mrs Osei all day yesterday, so I still haven't apologized for what I told Zarrish.

"Hey," I say, looking at my watch. It's ten minutes until the morning bell rings and Isaiah is still upstairs sewing bin bags together for Mrs Osei's fashion show outfit.

"Mum, Isaiah is taking too long," I groan. Mum opens the kitchen door and Minnie flies straight past her towards Ryan. I manage to grab her before she runs out of the house. Minnie may only want to give Ryan a hug but if she gets out and sees a cat, we'll be chasing her all morning.

"Can I just go to school myself?" I ask, as Isaiah runs downstairs looking for Grandma's glue gun.

"No, you're not walking on your own," Mum says.

"She can come with me, Mrs Williams," Ryan says. Mum looks at Ryan and then at me.

"Alright, if you go together," she says, smiling. "Call me Diane, Mrs Williams makes me feel so old," she says with a laugh before closing the door. I leave Grandma's front garden and head onto the road with Ryan, who is riding his bike slowly beside me.

"Do you want to get on the back?" Ryan asks. I look at his bike, a small blue BMX with pegs at the back.

"No thanks," I say, continuing to walk.

"Go on, I don't want to stress you out because I know you hate being late, but you're going to be *really* late if you walk," Ryan says slyly. I've seen the way Ryan rides his bike but I don't want to be late and get another late mark.

"I'll be careful," he promises.

"You'll stay on the pavement?" I say. Ryan nods and, even though I don't entirely believe him, I jump on. I hold tightly onto his shoulders as he speeds through Chorlton Park and back onto the pavement.

"Slow down, Ryan," I say as he swerves round people, narrowly missing them.

"What? I can't hear you," he says.

"Slow down!" I yell louder. He doesn't hear me and continues to ride as fast as he can. I have no choice but to close my eyes, not wanting to see the destruction unfold in front of me. Then I feel the bike come to a sudden halt. I'm scared to open my eyes but when I do, I'm relieved to see that we're in the schoolyard.

"Didn't you hear me shouting?" I ask as he locks his bike up.

"Yeah, I did," he laughs.

"Ryan!" I say, shocked that he didn't even try to lie to me.

"What? You said you didn't want to be late," he says. "Besides, if you forgot about being worried for just a second, you'd admit that you actually enjoyed it."

"Enjoyed you almost knocking over two old ladies?" I say, heading into school though the student entrance.

Ryan scrunches up his face. "They were *miles* away."

As we enter the student entrance, seeing Mrs Osei walk past reminds me of yesterday. "Hey, thanks for backing me up yesterday in the house office," I say, looking at my shoes, my face feeling warm. I wish I didn't have to lie to Mrs Osei. I wish I didn't have to hide in the toilets just to avoid going up to the front in assembly.

"Any time." He shrugs it off like it's no big deal.

"And Ryan," I say. I pause when Ryan turns round to look at me.

"Yeah?" he says.

"I'm the reason why Melissa knows about your mum. I didn't mean it like she said, but I'm really sorry."

He doesn't say anything as we continue walking inside. Was Isaiah wrong? Have I just made everything worse?

"It's fine," he finally says.

"Are you sure?" I ask.

He takes a deep breath and I regret asking. "Yeah, I know you didn't mean it in a bad way. I just don't want to talk about my mum, okay?"

"Okay," I agree. I'm curious to know more, but I drop it like Ryan wants me to.

"Wait, where are you going?" I ask, after Ryan begins walking in the opposite direction from our form room. "Er," Ryan says, scratching his chin. I've noticed that he does this when he's thinking – and that's usually thinking of ways to get out of telling the truth.

"I've got to go and see Mr Johnson," he says, rushing off. I wonder why he'd be seeing Mr Johnson when we don't have a music lesson today. But then I notice Zarrish sitting alone in the dining hall. Butterflies dance around in my stomach as I approach her. I shouldn't be nervous about sitting down with Zarrish, but as I reach her an awkward silence greets me.

"Do you want to go up to the hill at lunchtime?" I ask timidly. We always used to go up to the hill. The small mound that separates the field from the school gates is the perfect place to people watch. We stopped because there were too many people up to no good there and lunch would usually end with Mr Peterson and Ms Morrison shouting at everyone to move. But I'll go if it cheers Zarrish up.

"Don't you have athletics club at lunchtime?" she asks. She says it so coldly that it makes me look down at the table. I'm sure it will be fine if I miss it once. I'll do extra practice at home and can go again next week when things with Zarrish are better. I don't want to go another day with her being in a mood with me.

"It's fine, I don't have to go," I say slowly.

"Okay, cool," Zarrish smiles, finally making eye contact.

"Cool," I say.

"What's cool?" Melissa says, sitting down. She makes me move over to another seat to give her more room.

"We're going to the hill at lunch," Zarrish says.

"Melissa," I say. Melissa and Zarrish both look at me. I want to get the bad feeling over with before the fair. "I'm sorry for what happened in the house office."

Melissa pulls a face. "Do you think I care? We can't all be teacher's pets like you and your brother so don't worry about it, okay?"

"Okay," I mumble, wishing I hadn't said anything.

Everyone falls silent. The only noise comes from Melissa, who takes a bite of the toast she just took straight out of Zarrish's hand. For the first time, I'm not the only one who doesn't know what to say.

CHAPTER 19

After lunch, I look out of the window once I sit down in maths and see everyone from athletics club walking inside. Edie and Razan are walking slowly, holding relay batons in each hand. Guilt sweeps over me as I remember the messages on our group chat about practising for our relay race. I'm disappointed that I've missed it, but at least Zarrish doesn't seem to be in a mood with me since we sat on the hill. She spent most of her time on her phone or talking about the fair, which is getting closer and sounding less fun every time we talk about it.

"Has Ryan arrived yet?" Ms Morrison asks, walking into the classroom.

"Not yet," Mr Adams replies. They talk in hushed tones but I just about make out that he's on "thin ice" for ripping up the posters on the music corridor. Why would he do that?

He loves music and gets on well with Mr Johnson. He even went to see him before form time today. Something must've happened. I know that Ryan has his own way of dealing with things and it never ends well. He's going to get into more trouble for skipping maths, then he's going to get into even *more* trouble for reacting to being in trouble. It's a never-ending cycle. Plus, he's on the yellow report. Maybe this was his last chance. Maybe it's already too late.

I have to find him before Ms Morrison does. I take a breath, knowing what I have to do. "Yes, Storm?" Mr Adams says, shocked to see my hand in the air for the first time this year, and disappointed when I ask him if I can go to the toilet instead of answering the question he just asked the class.

He writes me a note and I leave the class with my head down as everyone watches, bemused by my actions. I have no idea where I'm going; I just know that I have to find Ryan, and fast.

I check the sensory garden and the bike sheds, but he's nowhere to be found. Where would you hide if you didn't want anyone to find you? My stomach feels heavy realizing where he could be. If I go in there, I'd be breaking a school rule. But if I don't, I can't speak to Ryan and he'll get kicked out of school. I don't have a choice. As I approach the Bistro, I stop and freeze. A cleaner is still clearing up in the dining hall. How am I supposed to get past now? I pretend to be walking through until the cleaner turns the other way. Now is my chance. I look around to make sure the coast is clear, before diving head first inside the Bistro. I stop dead at the sight of Ryan sat down on the floor by the window, then I cross over to him and sit down beside him.

"Do you want to hear a joke?" I say, breaking the silence.

"Go on then," he sniffles. Is he crying?

"What do you call a fake noodle?"

Silence.

"An impasta."

I wait for a moment before explaining.

"I get it," he says quietly.

"I know, it's lame. My mum told me to use it when I started athletics club as a way to make friends. I didn't, of course, that would have been very embarrassing."

I stop talking when I think I hear someone coming, but the noise soon fades away.

"So why are you in here?" I ask.

"I was supposed to start guitar lessons today at break time but when I went up to music, Mr Adams was on duty by the stairs and he wouldn't let me past. He said he didn't believe that I had a guitar lesson and said he reckoned I just wanted to cause trouble."

"Didn't you have a note?" I ask.

"I lost it. I said I would go get another one after but he wouldn't let me through. He said there's no way *I* could have a guitar lesson. It made me mad because my grandad had already paid for it. Then Ms Morrison had to come and stick her beak in, didn't she? I stormed off and then when the bell went for lesson, I decided to go back up to music to explain to Mr Johnson why I missed the guitar lesson, but he said he was teaching and that I had two more strikes before my lessons are cancelled. I got angry and ripped up the corridor. He'll probably ban me from music now, but I guess that's the least of my problems as I'll have one more strike on this," he says, taking out his yellow report and throwing it as far away as he can.

He stops talking and the room is silent until he speaks again.

"I don't want my grandad to get sick of me like my mum did."

"He won't," I say. From what I overheard Grandma telling Mum, I know that the reason for Ryan living with his grandad isn't anything to do with Ryan at all.

"Can't you just explain what happened?" I say.

Ryan shakes his head. "What's the point? Nobody ever believes me. Besides, I did rip off the notices and kick over a few bins."

"Yeah," I say trying to think of a way for Ryan to get out of this.

"Hang on," he says. "What are you doing in here?" He looks at me as if he's only just realized where we are.

"I'm here looking for you! Every senior member of staff is out there searching for you," I say, instantly regretting sharing that information. Ryan puts his head down again. "If we just go back to lesson and you do the work, then at least they can see that you haven't spent the rest of the day truanting. You can explain your side of the story when Ms Morrison does eventually find you," I explain.

"No," he says.

No? I've just lied to a teacher, again – and done so in front of the entire class – to find him. He can't say no. "I'm not saying you're going to be let off. I'm saying that if you go back to lesson before a teacher finds you, then you won't be in *as much* trouble."

He doesn't respond for a while.

"Mr Adams will only send me straight out," he says.

"No, he won't. Ryan, trust me. It's better than staying in here for Mr Peterson or Ms Morrison to come and find you."

"Fine," he finally agrees. I stand up before he changes his mind. We make sure the dining hall is empty before running out of the Bistro as quickly and as quietly as possible. I decide to walk in to maths first, trusting that Ryan will follow shortly after. He does and we both sit down at our table. Mr Adams continues teaching the lesson, completely ignoring the fact that I spent fifteen minutes out of lesson and that Ryan has only just walked in. I hand Ryan his worksheet, giving him a small smile.

"Cheers," Ryan whispers.

"Any time."

CHAPTER 20

I look up at the trees that fill the sky. Mr Harris makes us do this after we cool down at the end of athletics club. I take deep breaths looking at the shapes of the leaves. Since I missed athletics club to make things right with Zarrish, I've been training all morning to make up for it. I've decided I'll give Mr Harris's cool-down meditation a try, but I've not been on the ground for two minutes before Minnie pounces on top of me.

I give up and head back inside, hoping no one is in the bathroom, as I need to get ready.

It's Saturday afternoon and I'm going to the funfair with Zarrish and Melissa later on. The thought of getting a makeover from Melissa fills me with dread, but I know that it will be worth it. Once we're at the fair, everything will be alright. Nobody can resist the joy of going on rides until you're dizzy and eating too many sweets, not even Melissa. By the end of the fair, she will see why I'm Zarrish's best friend. It's my chance to prove myself.

I hear the music blasting from the fair as I walk to Zarrish's house. The smell of the fair brings back memories and I feel excitement rush over me as I knock on Zarrish's front door.

"Storm, it's so good to see you," Mrs Asif smiles as she opens the door. "I've missed you around the house," she continues as I step inside. "It's good that you two are still keeping your traditions. I've made lots of food for the sleepover later so don't eat too much candyfloss!"

I walk up the stairs to Zarrish's room. Her door is closed and there's a new neon sign that reads *PRIVATE, NO ENTRY* so I knock and wait.

"Go away," Zarrish shouts. "It's Storm," I call back and the door swings open.

"Sorry, I thought you were my mum," she says, letting me in.

I look around her room. It's changed so much since the last time I was in here. She's taken down her gymnastics ribbons and the lava lamp that I got her for her birthday, and she now has a photograph of her and Melissa in a frame that says *Besties* on it.

"Storm, sit here," Melissa says, ushering me towards a chair.

I hide my hesitation as Zarrish begins squirting some of her mum's foundation onto a brush before splurging it across my face. Melissa and Zarrish take it in turns to apply blusher and eyeshadow to my face. I look in the mirror and gasp. I don't recognize my own face. My freckles have been erased and I have eyeliner sprawled across my eyelids. Even my lips have been made bigger with red lip pencil.

"Okay, now it's time for the clothes," Melissa says reaching for her bag.

"Clothes?" I say. I totally forgot about needing a new outfit.

"Yeah, we're all matching," she says, throwing a strapless pink dress at me. "Mum took me on a shopping spree after I kicked off about Mrs Osei putting me in the exclusion room." I have to stop myself from saying it, but if I ever dared to kick off at my parents, I wouldn't get new clothes. I would get grounded.

I look down at the blush-pink dress and back up at Melissa.

"Well, say thank you. I didn't have to get you one, but we didn't want you to feel left out, did we, Zarrish?"

I look towards Zarrish, who is too busy faffing around with plug sockets for her hair straighteners to get involved.

"I could've got a new bag or something. You should've seen what I got after I left St Margaret's," she boasts rummaging through Zarrish's jewellery box.

"Did something bad happen? I heard St Margaret's isn't very nice," I say. When I told Isaiah that Melissa was from St Margaret's he almost fell out of his chair. He explained that it's usually for kids who've been kicked out of another school.

Melissa shrugs. "I got kicked out."

My eyes widen. "Kicked out?" I ask. "For what?"

"Just stuff," she says, turning her attention to Zarrish's make-up. A purple drop of nail varnish lands on the floor. Melissa shrugs and turns in the other direction. I watch Zarrish, looking worried, but she doesn't do anything, so I quickly take a wipe to clean it up. I'm starting to wonder if Zarrish is scared of Melissa.

I also wonder what she must have done to get kicked out of St Margaret's. I mean, who gets kicked out of school after only two terms? My questioning comes to an abrupt end when Melissa decides that it's time to get changed. I quickly put on the dress and cringe at myself in the mirror. I can't go out like this.

"I'm not too sure about the dress?" I say, slightly worried. The strapless pink dress is short and super tight and while it might be fine with Melissa and Zarrish, it's not something that I would ever pick out for myself. It's like they have moulded me into a completely different person.

"We'll look so much better in photos if we all look the same," Zarrish says, explaining why she isn't backing me up.

"Do we have to teach you everything?" Melissa sneers. "Besides, that dress was expensive. It's not our fault if you don't have style."

I agree to wear the dress so they can stop explaining fashion to me. I try my best to sit down, but the dress is too restrictive so I stay where I am, rummaging through my bag as a distraction while I try to think of how to get out of this night.

"What are those?" Melissa asks.

She reaches into my bag and takes out my pyjamas. "Llama pyjamas?" she smirks, holding up my pyjamas against me. "Quick, let me take a picture of Storm with her baby pyjamas."

I try to move, but she demands that I keep still. She takes a picture before flinging my pyjamas back to me. I look at my baby-blue matching set with a llama with sunglasses on and push them back in my bag. I didn't even think when I put them in my bag, but I am deeply regretting my decision.

"Can you delete that?" I ask, watching Melissa laugh into her phone at the photos that she just took of me.

"Melissa?" I say, raising my voice enough for her to look up from her phone. "Can you delete the photos, please?" I repeat, surprised at my own voice that is louder this time.

Melissa rolls her eyes. "Alright, geez, you're so boring sometimes." She holds up her phone. "Look, I've deleted them. Happy now?"

"Relax, Storm, it's just banter," Zarrish says. I try to fix my face so I don't show that I'm upset. I focus on the posters on the wall to stop my watery eyes from showing.

"Let's go," Zarrish suggests, noticing the tension in the room. Saying goodbye to Zarrish's mum, we head out of the door.

"Choose a song, Storm," Zarrish says handing me her phone. I think for a moment about what they would like. I try to think back to the music Melissa blares out of her phone at lunchtimes.

"You're taking too long," Melissa says, grabbing the phone from my hand.

We carry on walking and I zone out from their gossip. My mood lifts slightly at the sound of the fair getting louder.

"Shall we go in the haunted house first? Remember last year when we made it all the way without running away in the other direction?" I ask, laughing at the memory of us being scared of the pretend bats and strange howling noises, until we noticed the zombie running round was wearing Adidas trainers, giving it away that he was the man from the ticket office. Zarrish smiles gently at the memory.

As we get to the entrance gates of the park, Melissa stops.

"Let's go to town instead," she says.

"What? But what about the fair?" I say, panicking as Melissa and Zarrish both walk past the park gates.

"The fair is boring," Melissa says. She turns to look at Zarrish. "Let's go to town, it'll be way better."

I'm not allowed to go to town on my own, especially not at this time.

"I won't be allowed," I say. I'm pretty sure Zarrish isn't allowed either.

"First you're not allowed to the Trafford Centre and now town. Are you pretending or are you really this tragic?" Melissa snaps at me before turning her attention to Zarrish.

"Are you coming, Z?" she says, already walking away like she knows the answer.

I run to try and catch up with Zarrish, who is following Melissa to the bus stop into town. "But what about the rides? And the candyfloss?" I say to Zarrish, trying to remind her of the things we used to love about the fair.

"We should have given you a personality makeover as well," Melissa smirks.

I look at Zarrish who has suddenly gone quiet. Why is she always silent when I need her the most?

"Come on, Zarrish. Why are you even friends with her?" Melissa says. "Just tell her now what you were going to tell her days ago."

I can see Zarrish thinking this through. Melissa grows impatient at her hesitation.

"Look," Melissa continues. "We tried to give you a chance but you failed. Zarrish doesn't want to be your friend any more, do you, Zarrish?" she says. My breath catches in my throat as I fight the tears starting to fill my eyes.

"No, I don't," Zarrish finally says. "Just go and make your own friends, Storm."

Melissa smiles proudly at Zarrish before looking me up and down. I turn round and run. I run as fast as I can, not looking back. I just keep running.

CHAPTER 21

"Earth to Storm," Edie says, waving her hand in front of me.

I look round to see Edie, Razan and Teija all staring at me.

"Are you alright?" Razan asks.

"Me?" I say.

"Yeah, you seem antsy," Edie quizzes me.

It's Monday lunchtime and I'm sat with Edie, Razan and Teija on the field. Edie texted me yesterday to say that we're practising for our relay race every day until the finals, so I had no choice but to come out to meet them, especially since I missed club last week. I'd wanted to make it up to Zarrish, which was a waste of time because she isn't even my friend any more. I had hoped that we could practise in the sports hall, but the Year Nine basketball team got there before us. Razan volunteered to steal their ball so they couldn't play, but Edie and Teija overruled her.

I turn round from looking over at Zarrish and Melissa, who are sat by the benches.

"I'm fine," I lie.

I haven't seen Zarrish since I ran away from her and Melissa on Saturday. When I walked to form this morning I avoided all areas where she could be, but I can't avoid her now. I haven't told anyone about them falling out with me. When I got in on Saturday, I rushed straight upstairs before anyone could see me and got changed out of Melissa's clothes. I quickly washed my face before telling Mum and Dad that I came home early because I didn't feel well. One reason why I haven't told anyone is because I think that Zarrish will change her mind. We've always been best friends. We know each other's secrets, we've been on holiday with each other's families, know when each other feels sad. How can she not want to be my friend any more?

"Okay, can we get back to choosing our name?" Razan says clapping her hands. "Every great team has one," she informs us.

"The US gymnastics team called themselves The Fierce Five in 2012 and The Final Five in 2016," Edie says thinking of ideas.

"Okay, The Fierce Four," Teija suggests.

Razan dismisses the idea immediately. "No, we can't just

copy someone else's name," she says. "What do we all have in common?" Razan asks. We all sit in silence thinking.

"Storm?" Edie asks. "Are you sure you're okay? You seem quiet," she says.

"I'm always quiet," I mutter. I blush, instantly embarrassed. All three of them are staring at me worriedly.

"I don't mean that type of quiet, I mean quiet like you're upset about something," Edie explains.

"I'm fine," I say. "It's just hot." Edie shuffles over and I move closer into the shade.

"Hair!" Razan suddenly blurts out.

"You want us to be called hair?" Teija asks.

"No, we all have curly hair! How did I miss that?" Razan says. I look at each of them. It's true, we all do have curly hair, except Razan's is kinkier and Edie's is wavier. Teija has the same hair texture as me, except her curls have blonde tips that my mum would never let me have.

"Okay, Curly Girl Gang, let's practise!" Razan says happily standing up.

I look over at Zarrish and Melissa on the benches and hesitate. I can't race while they're watching.

"It's busy on the field, I don't think there's enough room for us to practise properly. Maybe we should go inside the sports hall?" I say, trying my best to think of a way out of this.

"The basketball team are in there, remember?" Edie says.

"But—"

Not letting me finish my sentence, Razan links my arm as we walk over to the track.

"We haven't got time to mess about, let's do this," she says.

"Storm, you should be the anchor," Edie decides. I turn to look at her with dread. The anchor on a relay team is the person who runs last. I look at the track and notice that this means that my lap of the race will be right next to the benches, exactly where Zarrish and Melissa are.

"I think Teija should go last. Can I go second?" I say, not wanting to stand close to the crowd watching.

"But you need to be the anchor because you're the fastest. You will be the best at making up ground against our competitors," Razan explains, agreeing with Edie.

"I'm not! I came third, remember?" I say.

"You only came third because you panicked. You have us with you now," Edie says, trying her best to encourage me.

"We're the Curly Girl Gang! Nobody can stop us," Razan says jostling me to walk into position.

All three of them are looking at me quizzically as I remain still. I don't want them to think I'm totally weird, so I nod and head towards my spot by the benches, making the mistake of looking over to see Melissa and Zarrish watching us. Razan counts us in.

"On your marks. Get set. Go."

Edie sets off running down the track line, so quick it almost takes me by surprise. She holds the baton towards Teija, who snatches it before sprinting off. She strides down the track and passes the baton to Razan, who runs towards me. When I step up to run, I glance towards the crowd forming next to Melissa and Zarrish. Why are they all watching? Razan shouts at me to start running and it catches me by surprise.

"Take the baton," she yells. I grab the baton but it slips from my fingers and onto the ground. "Storm!" Razan says, struggling to hide her disappointment.

"I'm sorry," I say, not daring to look over to the crowd.

"It's alright, we'll go again," Razan says. "Don't worry, you'll get it this time," she adds when she notices I look deflated.

Razan counts Edie in again and I close my eyes and take deep breaths.

"On your marks. Get set. Go."

I try to remember Mr Harris's advice. I don't look around me this time, I don't even look behind to see if Edie has passed the baton to Teija yet. I jump at the sound of my name.

"Storm, start running," Razan says. I do what she says and

begin to run. When I turn round to see her, she's already right beside me holding the baton out in her hand. I reach my hand backwards and put a firm grip on it. "Yes, Storm!" Razan shouts as I pull away with the baton in my hand.

"Go, Storm!" I hear Teija shout.

I turn to see the crowd but all that I can see is Melissa and Zarrish whispering to each other. Why are they there? How could Zarrish change so much since Melissa arrived? How could they be so mean? My mind is swirling like it's having a race of its own. All of a sudden, my feet become jumbled and as much as I try to stop myself, suddenly I'm face down on the ground.

"Are you okay, Storm?" Edie says. I'm still on the floor as the Curly Girl Gang crowd round me. I don't know what's worse, the pain that's throbbing in my ankle or the fact that I'm now surrounded. I've never been good with people surrounding me, I just feel more worked up. I try to stop the flow of tears from rushing down my face, but I can't seem to control it. At the sound of the bell I hear Mr Harris shout at everyone to move away, then call for help using his walkie-talkie. I'm still on the ground when Mr Harris tells Edie, Razan and Teija to go too. They leave the baton with him and follow the rest of the crowd indoors. My stomach flips as Mr Harris looks down at my ankle with way too much concern on his face.

"Can you point your toes?" he asks. I can but it hurts, badly. Mrs Osei heads over with a wheelchair from first aid. I pull myself onto the chair and they wheel me inside. I keep my head down. I can't believe I've given Melissa another reason to make fun of me.

"What happened to you?" Koko asks as I'm wheeled into the medical room. Miss Scott looks worried too. The teachers leave the medical room leaving only me and Koko. Her levels must be high because she is slowly sipping water. From spending time with Koko, I'm starting to understand a lot more about diabetes and I can usually tell when she is feeling high or low.

"What happened?" Isaiah says, sticking his head round the door and frowning. Someone must have told him what happened because he looks like he just rushed out of lesson.

"I fell on the field. It was so embarrassing," I say, my face burning as I think about it again. I try not to remember the look on Melissa's face as I fell.

"You don't have to get worked up about it," Isaiah says. His nonchalant attitude only makes me more upset.

"It's alright for you, Mr Perfect. You've never done anything humiliating before. Everyone will be laughing at me. I'm never racing again," I sniffle.

Isaiah kisses his teeth. "Why do you keep calling me Mr Perfect?"

I shrug, not knowing what to say.

"You know I was bullied when I was in Year Seven, right?" he says.

"What?" I say looking up, surprised.

"People called me all sorts. Swot, teacher's pet, nerd. But you know what? I didn't care, because I'm confident in who I am. Yes, I like robotics and debating and running these charity events and why shouldn't I? So I stayed true to myself and look at me now – I'm the coolest!" he says, popping his collar. Koko and I glance at each other before we all burst out laughing. He walks over to me and puts his hands on my shoulders. "Imagine if I stopped doing what I liked because of what other people think, or Mum and her mates stopped roller-skating in the street, or Dad stopped playing in his band. Imagine what you can achieve if you stop caring about the opinion of others."

"Exactly," Koko joins in. "If I cared what people think about me, then there would be no Koko Sato and how lame would the world be then?"

"Right, Koko, it's lesson time," says Miss Scott, walking back in as Isaiah heads out, giving my shoulders a final squeeze before he goes.

Why didn't I know that Isaiah was bullied when he was in Year Seven? He's always the first person to break up fights in the schoolyard, or to stand up for someone who's being pushed about. I could never imagine him as the one being bullied.

As Koko and Miss Scott leave for lesson, I'm told to wait for my dad, who is coming to pick me up. Even though my foot is throbbing, I'm relieved that I get to leave school. At least I won't have to see anyone for a while.

"Aww, llama girl is all alone," I hear a cold voice call out to me. I look up to see Melissa standing in front of me. Llama girl? It takes me a minute to figure out what Melissa is saying. I totally forgot about my pyjamas. "It was so embarrassing watching you on the field! I'm glad everyone got to witness what a loser you really are. To think Mrs Osei signed you up for the relay team! I might actually turn up to Sports Day now, it's going to be hilarious."

I keep my head down, not saying a word. "Teija isn't your friend by the way. I hope you realize that. She's going to see that you're a loser. Just like Zarrish did." I breathe slowly, trying not to let Melissa get to me. "Bye, llama girl," she chants as my dad's car finally pulls up outside.

* * *

I spent two hours in accident and emergency to find out that I twisted my ankle. Mum says that I have to rest it if I'm still to compete in the championship finals next week. I look at my phone to see messages from the Curly Girl Gang then quickly put my phone down, not wanting to read them. What happens if I can't compete in the championships? I thought falling over in front of everyone would be the worst feeling in the world, but the thought of not competing in the championship finals is even worse. I've lost my best friend, let down the relay team and now maybe I have lost the chance to represent Daisy Mill in the finals too. The thought of everything falling apart makes my stomach hurt, so I hobble into the kitchen and sit down at the table. Mum puts ice cream in front of me and I instantly feel better, until I notice a weirdness in the air. I put my spoon topped with chocolate ice cream back in the bowl slowly.

"Where's Minnie?" I ask. "Has she been banished to the garden again?" I turn round to see if I can see her out of the window, but she isn't there. Mum and Dad look at each other nervously. Thinking about it, they've both been acting strange all afternoon. Dad wasn't playing music in the car on the way home and Mum shouldn't even be here; she's normally at work at this time and she wasn't wearing her uniform. Did she even go in today?

"What's going on?" I ask, not sure if I want to know the answer.

"It looks like we're going to have to stay at Grandma's for a while longer," Mum says, sitting down at the kitchen table. This isn't news. Mum and Dad have been moving more of our stuff here all week so it's not like a big secret. Why are they being weird?

"You know, Minnie is too boisterous for your grandma, so we have decided that Minnie should stay with your Auntie Gemma, just until we move back home."

It takes me a minute to process what Mum has just said.

"It will be better for Minnie too. Auntie Gemma has a huge garden and can spoil her rotten. It'll be like she is on holiday," Dad says, trying to make it better. But it doesn't, nothing will.

"But Auntie Gemma lives in Bury, that's ages away! You can't just take Minnie to Bury without telling us," I sob.

"We can go visit at the weekend, and, Storm, it's only until we move back home," Dad says, but his words fail to make me see any differently.

"You can't just send her away!" I jump up and ignore the throbbing pain in my foot as I make my way out of the kitchen.

"Storm, come back," Mum calls after me.

I ignore her as I slam the kitchen door behind me.

CHAPTER 22

I can't go in.

I'm back at school after Mum let me stay off for two days. I think that was only because she felt bad about sending Minnie to stay with Auntie Gemma. No matter how much I kicked up a fuss, Mum and Dad wouldn't change their minds. "It's for the best" and "It's only a temporary arrangement" were the phrases they both repeated.

I came downstairs this morning to breakfast made by Mum, even though she had a night shift. Dad offered to give me a lift to school, but I left the house without taking a bite out of Mum's famous pancakes. Now that my ankle is feeling much better than it did, I walked to school with Isaiah, who was equally as upset, but less vocal about getting Minnie back. I think he agrees with Mum and Dad.

Now I'm stood alone in the corridor outside of my form

room because I'm too scared to go in. What if everyone is talking about my fall? I tried to not think about it, but now the memory of my legs tangling and crashing to the ground is on replay in my mind.

My legs start to tremble as I peer through the classroom window. Mr Adams has the class playing a game of charades as he marks maths books frantically.

"What you doing?" Ryan says, causing me to jump. I turn round and see him walking towards me.

"Are you back in lessons?" I ask, realizing I don't know how much trouble he got into for damaging the music corridor at lunchtime last week.

"Ms Morrison has put me on lunchtime detention for a whole week, but said she won't write it on my report. I've got one last chance," he says, opening the door and giving me no choice but to follow him inside.

"Storm's here," he says, announcing my reluctant arrival as he crashes down in his seat.

"Carry on with your game," Mr Adams orders, continuing with his marking.

"It's my turn," Abdul says. He gets up and walks to the front of the classroom. I feel a slight relief as the class go back to playing charades. Abdul thinks for a moment. He always takes ages to think of something. He scans the room for ideas. He looks at me and smiles widely. "Okay, who am I?" Abdul says. He runs to the other side of the classroom. His arms jump in the air before he falls to the floor. Laughter fills the room and my cheeks go bright red. "You're Storm!" Grace sniggers.

"Shut up, Abdul, you're so annoying," Ryan snaps.

"And you can stop smirking too! As if you haven't done anything totally embarrassing before," Koko turns to Grace.

"Yeah!" Ryan chimes in.

Koko and Ryan are locked in an argument with Grace's table as Mr Adams stays oblivious.

"Are you okay, Storm?" Asha whispers. I nod yes but I want the ground to swallow me whole. I try my hardest to fight the tears that want to stream down my face as Mr Adams asks everyone to settle down, before continuing with marking. I don't want to look up in case anyone sees my red puffy eyes, so I keep looking down, gripping my bag tightly.

At lunch, I weave through the sea of green blazers and packed tabletops, making my way to an empty space by the windows. I was late out of period four because Ms Morrison kept us behind after Ryan knocked over a box of measuring tubes, which smashed into tiny little pieces that took the science technician the rest of the lesson to pick up. Ryan swore that he was pushed into them by Abdul, who went on to protest his innocence from the other side of the classroom.

Ms Morrison didn't seem to care who caused the measuring tubes to fall. She decided to keep us all behind to lecture us for what felt like the millionth time. Since I have to rest my foot, so I'm fit enough to compete in the championships next week, Edie and Razan said they'd meet me in the dining hall. We were texting all the time when I was at home. I don't match their confidence in my ankle getting better in time for the championships, but I still agreed to meet them so they can help me think of a nickname for my hoody. Mr Harris needs to send the designs off today if we're going to get them in time. They probably think I'm off today or got bored waiting and now I'm sat alone eating a watery Jamaican brown stew chicken.

I take a bite out of the thick, soggy rice before putting my fork down in disgust. Before I can take my tray back and escape, Mrs Osei's walkie-talkie hits the table and I look up to see her smiling face, made brighter by her purple lipstick, as she sits down opposite me. Her Aztec-style earrings swing fiercely as she does so.

"I've been thinking about who should be the flag-bearer for Sports Day and I would like you to do the honours." Mrs

Osei puts her hands on the table, only just missing the blobs of tomato ketchup and orange juice spillages left behind after the lunchtime rush.

"Me?" I say, eyes wide.

Isaiah has told me all about the flag-bearer. It's a huge responsibility, because Sports Day is one of the biggest days of the school year. All the competitors are led out of the sports hall onto the field to excited applause, and the person carrying the house flag leads the way. Mrs Osei wants that to be me. The girl who fell flat on her face two days ago.

"I—"

I don't know what to say. I mean, how amazing would it be to lead my entire house out on the biggest day of the school year? On the other hand, I will be leading the way, which means I'll be first. There's no hiding when you're first. An echoing voice from Mrs Osei's walkie-talkie shouts that she's needed for an incident near the music room and she stands up, patting down her floral pink dress.

"Can you let me know by the end of the week?" she says, before leaving the table and striding through the dining hall towards music.

I take out my phone to write a reminder, not wanting to forget anything for Mrs Osei, when my home screen flashes up a picture of Minnie and makes my heart sink. I go to pick up my tray but before I can get up, Mr Adams drops a handful of orange exercise books on the table, sitting down where Mrs Osei just left. I don't tell him that he just put the books on top of a blob of tomato ketchup.

"Hi, Storm, can I have a quick word?" he says, adjusting his red Manchester United tie as he waits for my response.

"Yes, sir," I say, hesitantly putting my tray back down.

"It's just your maths assessment grade isn't as high as I had hoped. It's below target, I'm afraid. Do you think it would be a good idea if we arranged for you to have some maths support sessions with one of our sixth-form maths tutors?"

I tap my foot in panic. Maths sessions with a sixth former? That sounds awful. Mr Adams is looking at me to respond but as soon as I've found my voice, he cuts me off.

"Don't worry, I'll get everything sorted."

He disappears into the Bistro and I sit motionless for a moment.

"Aww, what's up, llama girl? Nobody will sit with you so you need teachers to? That's shameful!" Melissa shouts from the table nearest to the tray rack. "You're so tragic, llama girl."

I take a deep breath but it's failing to calm me down. Melissa is getting louder as her enjoyment in taunting me increases. "Here are your pyjamas," she exclaims, taking them from her bag and throwing them across the table. I forgot about my sleepover bag that I left at Zarrish's house. "I mean, who wears llama pyjamas at this age?" she continues loudly as people around her laugh. Melissa is lapping it up.

First, Zarrish replaces me with Melissa, then I embarrass myself by falling in front of everyone, Minnie gets banished to Auntie Gemma's, Mr Adams just told me that I have to spend more time doing maths and *now* Melissa is humiliating me again – this time in front of the entire dining hall. I stand up, gripping my tray firmly.

My brain is telling me to put down my tray and get out of the dining hall now. My feet, however, have other plans. They turn away from the tray rack and towards the taunts. The dining hall becomes blurry and all that I can hear is Melissa's voice, cackling loudly. I drop the tray on the table and pick up my plate. The Jamaican brown stew chicken swims in watery gravy that sways from side to side as I walk with purpose towards Melissa.

Zarrish's eyes widen and her mouth falls open as she points in my direction, but it's too late. My hands reach over Melissa as I pour my plate over her head. Melissa screeches as her hair is now dripping in brown stew gravy. The people around her jump up, not wanting to get covered in chicken juice, sending a ripple effect across the dining hall as everyone jumps up from their tables. Cheers and screams roar around the dining hall. I take a step backwards to turn round and run, but I bump straight into someone standing behind me.

"Storm Williams, come with me."

CHAPTER 23

I'm following Ms Morrison down the corridors, which suddenly feel narrow and impossible to walk down. For someone wearing high heels, she is walking with pace, clicking her fingers at me to walk faster. She's speaking into her walkie-talkie at high-speed, urgently muttering something about a Year Seven incident as several teachers in high-vis jackets rush past me towards the dining hall. My heart is pounding and I can hear blood rushing in my ears. I can only imagine Melissa's reaction right now.

"You alright, Storm?" Talia asks, scrunching up her legs that were blocking the corridor so Ms Morrison can walk past. Ms Morrison ignores both Talia and her non-uniform denim jacket and continues to power walk down the corridor.

Talia stands up and follows behind us. "What's happened, Storm?"

Ms Morrison doesn't let me reply to Talia as she says my name so sternly that I suddenly understand what it's like to be Ryan, trailing behind her, unable to explain myself.

"I'll go get Isaiah," Talia calls, turning round and running down the corridor. I don't think being Isaiah's little sister is going to get me out of this one.

Ms Morrison stands outside the exclusion room waiting for me to catch up with her before opening the door. I've never been inside the exclusion room before. When we had our school tour at the beginning of the year, Mr Adams skipped it, commenting that he didn't expect anyone in his form to be sent here. The door that Ms Morrison opened leads to a small entryway which opens out onto two classrooms. Ms Morrison snaps at me to wait as she makes her way inside the classroom on the right, shutting the door behind her. I wonder what happened after Ms Morrison escorted me out of the dining hall? I suddenly feel scared about what Melissa is going to do next. She's not going to let this go. I put my head in my hands as I imagine the entire school talking about me. Even the Year Tens and Elevens popped their heads out of the Bistro to see Melissa dripping in gravy.

"Storm, in here please," Ms Morrison calls, holding the classroom door open. The exclusion room is nothing like the prison I'd imagined it to be. There are no cells with bars, but two rows of tables with dividers instead, that split the tables into secluded workspaces, which I'm grateful for. I just want to be alone after my walk of shame. Ms Morrison walks over to Miss Callway, the exclusion-room manager, and from the way Miss Callway is nodding and staring at me, I know they're talking about me.

"Storm, you are going to be in here for the rest of the day," Ms Morrison explains. Ryan's head pops up from a divider and makes both Ms Morrison and Miss Callway jump.

"Storm? What are you doing in here?" he asks with a puzzled expression.

"Do I need to remind you of the exclusion-room rules? No talking and no looking out from your own work area," Ms Morrison snaps.

"But you've got it wrong, Storm couldn't have done anything! Who put you in here?" Ryan persists, turning to me. He continues to argue with Miss Callway and Ms Morrison. It's like watching a footballer argue with a referee who just awarded the other team a penalty.

A sharp buzzing from Ms Morrison's walkie-talkie makes her roll her eyes and she heads to the door. "I am very disappointed in you, Storm. What you did will have very serious consequences, including whether we can trust you to attend the athletics championship finals," she says looking directly at me.

"You can't do that!" Ryan says.

"One more word from you and you will be here for another week," Ms Morrison barks. Ryan falls silent and retreats behind his divider.

A pink sheet of paper is put in front of me by Miss Callway, titled *Incident Report Statement*. "Don't leave anything out," Miss Callway says, leaving me to write down my side of the story. Seeing the pink sheet overwhelms me. Everything rushes around in my mind, yet I have no idea where to start. However I try to write what happened down, I see no good way out. I'm in so much trouble. If my fall didn't end my chance at the championship finals, then this definitely has.

"Miss Callway, Storm couldn't have done anything," Ryan says again from behind his divider.

Miss Callway pauses before sipping her tea calmly and muttering, "She must have done something, because nobody gets escorted to the exclusion room by Ms Morrison for nothing."

There are five minutes left until the end of the day, when Miss Callway tells me to wait at the main reception for

Isaiah, who is being pulled out of class early to meet me. Ms Morrison thought it would best for me to avoid the end of day rush and keep away from Melissa.

"Here, Storm, I drew a picture for you," Ryan says, handing me a sheet of paper as I get to my feet.

With a lopsided tongue and mischievous glint in her eye, it had to be – "Minnie?" I whisper, staring at the sketch in my hands.

"I thought it would cheer you up," he says, shrugging it off and looking embarrassed.

I go to meet Isaiah but he's late as usual. I peer down at the picture of Minnie that Ryan drew for me. It has just given me an idea that will make me feel better.

With Isaiah still nowhere to be seen, I take it as my opportunity to make a run for it. As soon as I'm out of the school grounds and onto the street, I'm on a one-way mission to see Minnie, heading towards the tram stop without looking back. I reach into my pocket for coins before putting them into the ticket machine and quickly grabbing my ticket. I stand out of the way, nervously waiting for a tram that will take me to Bury. To Minnie.

The sight of the yellow tram getting closer fills me with relief, and I rush aboard as soon as the doors open. Jumping slightly as the tram jolts into movement again, I watch the tram stop get smaller and smaller until it disappears out of sight.

I've only been to Auntie Gemma's on the tram a few times and never by myself. The tram winds through street after street and I quickly lose track of where we are, peering out of the window to see if I recognize her street yet. This is much further than I remember. When it finally gets to my stop, it takes me a few minutes to know exactly where I'm going.

The time on my watch reads 5:30. I keep walking, passing neatly rowed houses with trimmed hedges and hanging flower baskets. I don't dare to look at my phone, because I know I'll have a zillion missed calls from Mum and Dad, so I have to think really hard to remember where I'm going. The shop on the corner becomes familiar and relief sets in. I'm on Auntie Gemma's street. I walk fast, until I'm running all the way to Auntie Gemma's house. *Minnie*. I finally see her, running in circles in Auntie Gemma's front garden. "Minnie!" I shout, opening the garden gate. Minnie stops circling and leaps at me so hard, it causes me to fall over. "Good girl, Minnie!" I shout as she joins me lying on the ground.

She barks so excitedly that Auntie Gemma comes rushing outside. "What's all the noise about?" Auntie Gemma calls, before looking up to see me lying in her front garden.

"Storm, thank goodness you're okay! Where have you

been? Everyone has been so worried," she cries, throwing her arms round me and leading me towards the house. "Come on, we best go inside and ring your mum and dad."

A few minutes later, Auntie Gemma comes out of the living room where she has just spoken to Mum and Dad on the phone. Sitting in silence, I watch as she puts the kettle on and potters round the kitchen.

"Here you go, Auntie Gemma's famous hot chocolate."

She puts a mug in front of me and sits down at the kitchen table. She takes a sip out of her own mug. "Go on then, Storm, tell me what's happened," she says, putting her drink down.

"Start from the beginning."

CHAPTER 24

Today I have to go back to school. I'm glad that my family know about what's been happening, but it doesn't make it any easier to go back in.

Mum and Dad gave me a stern talking-to for throwing my lunch over Melissa. Even though I caught Dad smirking as I explained how Melissa screeched when gravy dripped from her hair, they told me it wasn't the right way to deal with the situation and now I have to face the consequences head on.

Mum was fuming after I told her about Zarrish and the fair and how Melissa hasn't stopped making fun of me.

"Nobody bullies my daughter and gets away with it," Mum declared. She wanted to go straight in to school and sort it out herself. I had to persuade her not to. I told her that I could handle the situation myself.

Dad had been quiet as he listened to my story, frowning down at his hands, before turning to me and saying firmly, "No matter how quiet it is, you've got a voice, Storm. You should use it to speak up for yourself."

I have an official incident meeting today and, if I'm to believe Dad, now is the time to use my voice. I have to sit down with Melissa to resolve our differences before I'm allowed back to lessons. I bet she's going to spew her lies and play the victim like she always does.

"Are you sure you don't want us to come?" Mum asks, ready for me to change my mind.

"No, Mum," I say. "Besides, Mrs Osei is going to ring you later."

For once, Isaiah is ready to leave on time. He pulls me into a one-arm hug, giving my shoulder a squeeze as we head out. I stay extra close to him to as we walk into the school building and try not to think about how everyone is staring at me. Isaiah zooms forward when he notices Melissa on the corridor.

"No, Isaiah, don't," I plead, pulling his arm back.

"She needs a talking-to," he says, taking over from Mum in a bid to give her a piece of his mind.

"Can you not? People are staring. *Please*, Isaiah," I beg him, my face reddening as people turn to look. I manage to persuade him not to say anything as we walk past them to Ms Morrison's office.

"Have you seen what they're wearing?" Isaiah says, turning his head away from Melissa. I turn round and see Edie and Razan walking over to us. They're both wearing llama pyjamas over their school uniforms.

"Do you like them? I heard they're the new trend," Edie says with a grin and twirls. Razan strikes a pose next to her.

"You got here before me!" Teija calls excitedly as she spots us and jogs over. She is also wearing llama pyjamas that she has somehow managed to style.

"I can't believe that you would wear them to school," I say. I've been so worried about today, but seeing the Curly Girl Gang here, in my corner, makes me feel suddenly light.

"Listen, I dare Melissa to make fun of me," Teija says, grinding her fist into her hand.

"This is our way of telling everyone that we're on your side. If they want to make fun of you, they'll have to make fun of us too," Razan says, her eyes narrowed as she looks around, daring people to laugh.

"Curly Girl Gang for ever, right?" Edie says.

"We also have another surprise," Razan says excitedly. She pulls something out from behind her. "We got our hoodies made and they came yesterday."

"I forgot about them!" I say. After the incident with Melissa, I forgot all about choosing a nickname for myself.

"Don't worry, we thought of a nickname for you," Edie smiles, taking the hoody from Razan and passing it to me. I look at the back. There's a picture of a tornado on it with two trainers sitting on top. My nickname sits just under it. *Quiet Storm.*

"Do you like it? You're like a quiet storm because you come out of nowhere to beat everyone." They're all staring at me as I look down at my hoody. I love it.

"Thanks for coming up with the hoodies. I told everyone it was your idea," Teija says.

"Share more of your ideas in future, okay?" Razan says.

"Okay, I will," I say glumly.

"What's wrong?" Edie says.

"Ms Morrison said that I might not be allowed to go to the finals." I finally bolster enough courage to admit the full consequences to them.

"What?" Razan says a little too loudly. "She can't do that! We need you!"

"I'm *so* sorry. If I'd known I might be kicked off the athletics team, I would never have reacted to Melissa." I put my hands over my face in shame. It's not just me that I've ruined the finals for. If I'm not on the team, I can't compete in the relay which means I've ruined it for my friends as well.

"I understand if you don't want to be my friend any more. I have ruined the finals and made a total idiot of myself," I say.

"Even if they do decide that you can't run, we're still gonna be your mates," Teija says, tugging my arm.

"When you have your meeting, be honest and tell them everything. Ms Morrison can't punish you after she's heard what Melissa has done," Edie says confidently.

"And if that fails, text us and we'll be straight outside Ms Morrison's office to protest!" Razan says with determination in her eyes. I smile, knowing that Razan is being serious with her idea of starting a protest to get me back on the team.

I guess I do have friends. Friends who would dress in embarrassing pyjamas to make me feel better. Friends who pull each other up instead of putting each other down.

Ms Morrison's door opens and she waves me inside. "Don't forget, we're here for you, Storm," Razan says loud enough for Ms Morrison to hear.

Melissa walks in late and is ordered to sit opposite me, with Ms Morrison and Mrs Osei sitting in between us. I see both our incident report statements placed in front of Ms Morrison.

"Melissa, have you got anything to say to Storm?" Ms Morrison begins.

"Yeah, that she had no right to throw food at me and she's been jealous of me from the day I got here," she says. She folds her arms and pulls a face like she is ready for a fight.

I have no one here to stick up for me. No Ryan, no Koko or Curly Girl Gang. No Isaiah or Mum and Dad. I have to speak up for myself.

"Storm, have you got anything to say to Melissa?" All three of them are staring at me.

"I'm sorry that I splattered my lunch on you in front of the entire dining hall," I say.

Mrs Osei looks at me with a raised eyebrow.

"Okay, we're making progress. I think what we have to do now—" Ms Morrison says, shuffling the papers in front of her.

"I'm not finished yet," I interrupt, "I am sorry for what I did, and yes, Melissa, I was jealous of you when you arrived," I say. Melissa sits up straight and smirks as if to say, I told you so. "But you have been horrible to me for no reason. You're always putting me down and making fun of me and it isn't just me. You're horrible to loads of people, especially people in my form group. You said something horrible to Ryan that made him end up in trouble and you are always horrible to

Koko, really horrible. Just because Koko doesn't care what you say, it doesn't make it right. I'm sick of it. I snapped, but you would too if you had to deal with what you've been dishing out. Well, I'm not putting up with it any more," I say, sitting back in my chair with my arms crossed. Mrs Osei and Ms Morrison look at each other with their eyes wide. I'm not sure either of them has ever heard me speak so much.

"*Right*, okay—" Mrs Osei says slowly.

She fiddles with her pen for a second. "Is there anything that you would like to say, Melissa?" she asks. Melissa doesn't say anything. "I think an apology for the way you have been treating Storm would be a start," Mrs Osei says sternly.

"Sorry, Storm," she forces out.

"Not everyone gets along, but you are always to be respectful and civil, do I make myself clear?" Ms Morrison says. We both nod. Ms Morrison turns to me, "Storm, you head back to lesson," before turning to face Melissa, "and you wait here so we can address this further." I stand up, not cowering from Melissa as I leave Ms Morrison's office.

"And Storm?" Mrs Osei says, stopping me just before I open the door.

"Come by the Pankhurst House office at break time. I'm taking a group photo of all our participants for the championships for our newsletter."

My eyes widen. "But...?" I say, looking at Ms Morrison.

"After careful consideration, it's been agreed that you can still participate in the championship finals," Ms Morrison says.

The office door closes behind me and I want to breathe a sigh of relief, but as I start to walk away, I bump straight into Zarrish. We both stand frozen. She looks down at her shoes for a moment before looking up and muttering, "Sorry."

"For what?" I ask. I'm surprised by my own confidence but I stand tall and look directly at her expectantly. If I can stand up to Melissa, I can do this too.

"For going along with Melissa. I didn't want to break friends with you but she made me, she forced me to. She wanted me to ditch you ages ago but I kept saying no. I kept asking her to give you a chance, but she wouldn't listen." Zarrish steps backwards, wanting me to sit on the windowsill with her, but I stay where I am. She looks so unsure of herself. "I told her that you aren't all the things she said you were, but then you didn't want to meet us at the Trafford Centre and then you didn't want to go to town instead of the fair."

I really want to jump in and stop her, but I let her finish.

"Then you had those pyjamas and..." She scratches her head. "I told her you would change but it was too late, she blindsided me at the fair. What could I do?"

I think about the Curly Girl Gang and how they came into school wearing llama pyjamas just to make me feel better. I'm sure people will laugh at them but they didn't care, they had my back anyway. I don't need to change for them or prove how worthy I am.

"What about you, did you think I needed to change?"

She looks at me and bites her lip, hesitating before speaking. "I just wanted you to keep up. I wanted you to be more like us so we could have fun together. I wanted Melissa to see the real you, because I knew she would like you once she got to know you better. I just wanted you to stop being so shy. But it's all fine now, don't you see?" She's smiling now as she moves closer to me. "You've proven to Melissa that you have what it takes. Sure, you proved that by throwing your lunch all over her, but in a few weeks she'll get over it. I'm sure she'll see the funny side and we can all be friends next year when we're in Year Eight, you wait and see."

"Proven who I am?" I say, raising my voice. "You think I've proved myself by throwing my food over someone? That's not who I am. I don't go around having confrontations with people. Sorry if I didn't know that was the new way to make friends."

She takes a step back.

"I shouldn't have to prove myself to anyone or change

who I am. You wanted me to be friends with Melissa so much that you forgot to be my friend."

Her mouth drops open. "How have I not been a friend to you?"

Her response makes me laugh out loud, "Are you serious? If you'd paid attention you would know I'm going through a lot right now."

It's her turn to laugh now, which catches me off guard. What is she finding so funny? "Oh wow, so what, you have to share a room with Isaiah? Big deal."

"My family are actually really struggling right now. Not that you've even asked me about it once. And athletics?" I say, but she cuts me off.

"I didn't know you cared about athletics that much. You usually don't like those things because you're shy. I thought you would have given it up by now. Besides you're like Mrs Osei's favourite student now, so obviously you didn't need me."

"I've always been shy and I think I'm always going to be a bit shy, but I'm learning that it doesn't have to stop me doing the things that I like. When you didn't go to athletics I almost didn't go either, but I'm glad I did. I don't need you to be happy for me. I'm proud of myself and that's what matters."

"Well, good for you," she says, rolling her eyes. "Can we just stop arguing now and go back to how we were before the fair?" She's really not getting it and I'm tired of trying to explain. If she doesn't get that I don't have to change to fit in, then I don't want to be a part of whatever clique she wants me to change for.

"I'll see you around, Zarrish," I say, walking away. As I turn the corner, I take out my phone to text the Curly Girl Gang.

Storm: I'm back on the team!

I see three dots next to Razan's name.

Razan: YAY
Edie: Can't wait!
Teija: :):)

I put my phone away quickly, before a teacher walks past, and start to head to lesson.

I did it. I stood up to Melissa and Zarrish. Even though my stomach is churning and my face feels flushed from speaking up, I can walk away from both of them with my head held high.

CHAPTER 25

I wrestle my athletics hoody over my head, my thick black curls dancing as I scrape my hair back into a ponytail for what feels like the millionth time. Looking at my hoody, I notice that the lettering of my name glistens over my logo – a pair of trainers sitting over a tornado – which sends a wave of excitement and nerves so forcefully that I need to sit down at the bottom of Grandma's stairs.

It's the championship finals today and my mind hasn't stopped racing. I run my fingers round my ankle – it's much better now, but I've missed so many practices that I don't feel ready.

I'm snapped out of my thoughts as Mum calls me from Grandma's kitchen. I pull my phone out of my hoody pocket. It's 8:05, which means there's fifteen minutes before the morning bell and half an hour before the bus leaves for the finals.

"Storm!"

My name is echoing down the hallway again, so I hurry into Grandma's kitchen. "I'm going to be late!" I announce to Mum and Dad, who are both sat down at the kitchen table.

"Storm, love, you don't always have to be in such a hurry," Mum says, tapping the seat next to her. I reluctantly sit down, glancing up towards the clock.

"You're not going to be late, don't worry," Dad says sipping his coffee. I fiddle with the string pulls on my hoody, trying to relax.

"We know you struggle in social situations." I pull my hood over my head as Mum's words make me squirm. I sense one of her pep talks coming on so I hold my hands over my ears in embarrassment.

"No, listen. We know you find social situations hard but we're so proud of everything you have achieved. You've come such a long way," she says, also telling me to sit properly. I take my hood down reluctantly and look blankly at Mum and Dad.

"You've worked so hard, so we thought you deserved a special gift," Dad says, placing a box on the table. He slides it over to me and nods for me to open it. The box is hard to open but I manage it. I remove the gold tissue paper gently to reveal a brand-new pair of trainers.

"Just in time for the finals." Dad smiles.

I gasp, pulling the trainers out of the box. "Can you afford them with the house and everything?" I ask, admiring the pristine gold lace-up fastenings.

"What did I tell you? Stop worrying about the house, it's all sorted," Mum says.

"Now put them on, let's see if they fit," Dad adds.

I quickly kick off my shoes, before sliding my feet into the soft foam soles of my brand-new trainers. It's a perfect fit.

"Thank you so much!" I say, rushing over to give Mum and Dad the biggest hug.

"Hey." Isaiah yawns, coming into the kitchen.

"Finally, what took you so long?" I say, releasing my grip on Mum and Dad to finish tying my new shoelaces.

"I've been up all night creating this," he says, revealing a banner from behind his back.

"Oh my days, Isaiah!" I smile, looking at the banner that is coated in Daisy Mill colours. *Go Curly Girl Gang* is spray-painted on with gold and silver paint and sits just below a sketch of all four of us. We have our arms round each other, and a medal each round our necks. Isaiah has managed to capture each of our personalities. We all look different, but we fit together perfectly.

"You ready?" he says, grabbing his school bag.

I may have missed practices, but the support from my family and the courage I've had to stand up for myself may just take me over the line. I'm ready.

Manchester Regional Arena is a lot bigger than Longford Park, where we competed in the qualifiers. Warming up makes me feel like a real athlete, so much that I imagine myself sprinting down the track as if I've just won a gold for Team GB at the Olympics. I allow the excitement to override my fears and when the steward announces the Year Seven four-hundred-metres race, I take off my hoody and make my way to the starting line.

The tips of my toes go neatly behind the white line of my lane as the announcer asks for quiet. I get into my starting position and look ahead, focused.

"On your marks. Get set. GO."

The announcer sounds the bell and I hear cheers coming from every corner of the arena. I block out the noise and keep surging forwards. The cheers are soon drowned out by the sound of my feet pounding the floor as I run as fast as I can. I close my eyes as I dash down the final stretch, hoping it will make me go faster. I can do this, I tell myself. I can see the finish line and with one final stride, I cross it, slowing down into a jog until I'm able to stop, dropping down to the floor.

An unfamiliar face hovers over me and I manage to use the last of my energy to stand up. "Number 10, Daisy Mill Academy," the lady says while jotting something on her clipboard. "Congratulations," she smiles. "You're our first winner of the day."

Suddenly finding a boost of energy, I run to the Daisy Mill area where I'm met by a sea of green figures jumping up and down.

"YES, STORM!"

Teija leaps up, followed by Razan and Edie before I'm swarmed by all of my teammates.

"It's time to go to the podium," Mr Harris says, releasing me from the group celebrations.

My smile immediately drops from my face. I look at the podium taking centre stage in the middle of the track. My mind races as I remember the ceremonies from the athletics videos I've been watching on YouTube. The image of the winners standing on the podium with all eyes on them makes my legs tremble with fear.

"Go on, Storm!" Razan says, giving me an encouraging push forward.

"But—" I try to think of a way out of it until I notice the stand on the other side of the arena.

I can't believe it. I run to the stand, taking a giant leap into the crowd where Mum, Dad, Grandma and Mum's roller-skating club are all cheering wildly.

"What are you doing here?" I say. They're all trying to act as cool as ice now that I have spotted them.

"We wanted to come and support you," Tricia says.

"And we're on our best behaviour," Julie adds with a grin. I look at the banner that is in front of them. "GO STORM, GO" is written in big bold letters, just like they promised a few weeks ago.

"I hope you're not mad that we came," Mum says.

"Of course I'm not mad but –" they are all looking at me with held breath – "you're gonna have to cheer louder than that if we're gonna beat the St Margaret's relay team later on," I finish with a grin.

"Don't worry, Storm, we've got you," Grandma smiles. That I've never doubted.

"Now go have your moment," Dad says, pointing to the podium where everyone is waiting.

"But I'm scared of standing up in front of everyone," I say, tears starting to fill my eyes.

"Storm, look how far you've come. You deserve to stand

on that podium – don't let your fears stop you from realizing your dreams," Mum says.

"It's okay to be scared, but you can't let that stop you," Dad adds.

I look back towards the podium. Maybe I should just go for it.

"You can do it, love – it's not about us or anyone else watching. This is about you and what you've achieved," Grandma says, stroking my arm.

"Okay," I say, allowing their words to give me enough courage to walk steadily to the middle of the track. With my family watching on, I take a step onto the first-place spot on the podium. I look to the stands where Mum, Dad, Grandma and Mum's roller-skating club are beaming and then I look at the Curly Girl Gang, who are whooping loudly.

A gold medal is hung around my neck as I'm announced as the first-place winner of the Year Seven four-hundred-metres race. I lift my head up and look around to take in this moment. I don't know which is more surprising. The fact I have a gold medal after coming first in my race or that I'm able to stand here – centre stage with all eyes on me. Either way, I can't stop smiling. After everything – I did it.

I'm a champion.

* * *

"Whatever you do, don't drop the baton."

It's the final race of the day and it's been a close competition. A rumour has been going round that the final race will decide which school wins the championships, and I can feel the tension floating around the track. The Curly Girl Gang make our way to our positions for the final race of the day, the Key-Stage-3 relay race.

"Remember, if anyone drops the baton we are disqualified," Razan says. We all nod, knowing the consequences of letting the baton slip through our fingers.

"Look at the St Margaret's team. Why do they all look so scary?" Edie asks with a gulp. The St Margaret's team all look old enough to be in Year Eleven. They've been eyeing us up for the last hour and now they're already in position.

Edie pulls us all in for a group hug before we go our separate ways to our starting positions. My palms are sweaty as I can only think about the practice on the field at lunchtime, when I dropped the baton and ended up on the floor. It was decided that I was still going to be the anchor – which means that my lane is right in front of the crowd, who are waiting in anticipation. I can hear chants of "Let's go, Daisy Mill!" and "Let's go, Curly Girl Gang!" getting louder and filling my body with a rush of adrenaline. The announcer asks for quiet and, eventually, the crowd falls silent. The only things that I can hear are my thoughts that are on repeat.

Don't drop the baton. Don't drop the baton. Don't drop the baton.

"On your marks. Get set. GO."

I see Edie jump forwards at the sound of the bell. She takes the lead and passes the baton safely onto Teija, who sprints off ahead. The St Margaret's team are an inch away from her as she passes the baton to Razan. Racing ahead, Razan loses ground as the St Margaret's team edges closer until they overtake us. The final St Margaret's runner zooms past me. Razan inches closer, I rub my clammy palms onto my shorts, ready for the baton that she slots into my hand. I jet off down the track. I tell myself not to look round. *Focus on my own lane,* I tell myself over again. "Go, Storm!" I hear Razan roar as she slots the baton into my hand.

Yes!

I didn't drop the baton.

With the baton in my hand, I sprint. I don't think my body can go any faster but I don't give up, giving it everything that I have until I cross the finish line.

I drop to the ground as soon as I'm across the line. Three faces appear in front of me and pull me up instantly. "I can't believe it," Edie shouts, forming us all into a group hug. I can barely hear her over the cheers of the crowd.

"We won!" Teija screams, jumping up and down. Everything around me becomes blurry, like I'm in a dream. We won. I can't believe it.

"They're going to announce the championships – come on," she says as we rush back to the Daisy Mill area of the stands. My heart gallops at the sight of the big screen going blank.

We rush back to the athletics team in time for the announcement of the overall championship winners. It's going to be close between us and St Margaret's.

"The overall athletics champions are..."

I almost can't look. I pull my T-shirt up to my face and cover my eyes. I hear the screams before I look at the screen that has now changed to reveal the winners: DAISY MILL ACADEMY. I throw my arms round the Curly Girl Gang and we're joined by the entire athletics team. I see Mr Harris running towards us with his arms in the air and Mum's roller-skating club are now holding Isaiah's banner as they lead a synchronized dance in the stands.

Razan grabs my hand and we're all running to the podium. It's too small for us all to fit, but nobody cares as we all jump around in glee.

We did it.

We're champions.

After what feels like hours of celebration, I say goodbye to my family, who are already planning a special family night for when I get back home. Mum already sent Isaiah dozens of photos, to which he responded with a video of him, Talia and Princess cheering in the Bistro.

"Who wants to choose a song?" Razan says, passing her phone along the bus to Mr Harris. I sit down at the back, saving a space next to me for Teija.

I think about it before saying, "I've got one."

I instantly bite my tongue, but as my song blasts out from the speakers, Razan shouts, "This is a TUNE!" before the whole bus starts singing along.

CHAPTER 26

"We leave for crazy golf in half an hour," I say to Isaiah, who has just sat down with Grandma's sewing machine. It's the fashion show tomorrow and Isaiah has just about every teacher walking down his catwalk.

I'm getting ready for family night. Mum was so overly excited during the championship finals, that she invited the whole athletics team – including their families. Now we will be celebrating our win all night.

I've tried on at least five different outfits, but I've settled for a denim dress and Converse.

The doorbell rings and I rush downstairs. I thought everyone was meeting us at crazy golf.

"Ryan?"

Ryan stands on the doorstep with paint all over him. He congratulates me for winning the finals, but I'm distracted by the orange paint smudged on his face. With the excitement of the championships, I totally forgot about finishing the science homework project.

"It's due tomorrow and we still have two more planets to paint," I remember. We leave for crazy golf soon – there's no way we can do it.

"Actually I've just finished Mars and Venus," Ryan says, pointing to the paint splashed across his jumper. "So we're done."

"Well in that case, why don't you come to crazy golf with us?" Mum suggests, walking into the hallway.

"I would love that but I can't, because Grandad's stolen your idea," he says, grinning. I look at him questioningly. "We're having a family night, just me and him," Ryan continues. "We're going to the cinema. I wanted to watch the scary film that just came out, but Grandad said no because it's a fifteen, so we have to watch something else. I don't mind though – he says I can have a hot dog *and* popcorn."

"That's great, Ryan," I say, happy for him. "Thanks for telling me about the homework. I'll get my finished notes to you by the morning so we can go over them," I say.

Ryan scratches his head, "Cool. But that's not why I'm here. I came to see Isaiah."

I frown, "Isaiah?" What would Isaiah and Ryan have to talk about?

"Good, you're here," Isaiah says, rushing down the stairs and waving Ryan into the kitchen. I follow them curiously until Dad, walking out of the living room with his car keys in his hands, makes me stop.

"Where are you going?" I ask.

"I've got something to sort," Dad replies, putting his jacket on.

"I thought Williams family night needed every single Williams," I quiz him.

"I'll be back later," Dad promises, waving to Mum.

I watch Dad suspiciously as he gets into his car and drives off. Where could he be going on family night?

"STORM! UP HERE!"

I look up to see Razan waving to us from a table near the top of the escalators. It looks like everyone is already here as we make our way up to the entrance of crazy golf.

"The first group is Isaiah, Yasmin, Razan and Storm," Mum says, organizing everyone into groups.

"Get ready for war." Razan uses her golf club as a sword and leads the way inside.

"You're so extra, Razan," Yasmin says, trying to avoid being hit. Yasmin is Razan's younger sister, who will be joining us at Daisy Mill next year. She looks nervous as everyone around her chats in small groups.

"Have you ever played crazy golf before?" I ask her. She looks at me, seeming grateful that I started a conversation.

"Only once, but that was with my mum and dad on holiday," she says. "I'm Yasmin by the way, Razan's sister."

I smile. "I'm Storm, Razan's friend from athletics club."

The room darkens as we go inside. I push away leaves from the fake palm tree as we make it inside the first section. Razan goes first. Her swing is so brutal it sends the ball bouncing over the giant black taxi onto the jukebox and over the fake palm trees.

"Nothing to see here," she laughs, knocking over a cowboy mannequin as we make our way into the Wild West area.

"Hey, Isaiah," I say, catching him as he swats a palm tree to get ready to play.

"Thanks for handing in my qualifying letter," I say gratefully. If Isaiah hadn't handed in my letter to Mr Harris, there's no way that I would have gone through with the championships or even joined athletics club, which means that I wouldn't have had the chance to push myself and prove that I can do things, no matter how scary they are.

Isaiah smiles. "That's what big brothers are for, right?"

"You know what little sisters are for?" I ask, smiling as a crowd forms round us. "Beating you at crazy golf," I say, eyeing up where I need to hit the ball.

"Oh, it's on now," he says, measuring up his golf club. Everyone ducks out of the way to witness a classic Williams family night.

I will never be as outgoing or as outspoken as Isaiah, and that's okay. I'm coming to understand what he means when he tells me not to care about what other people think. I think back to what he went through when he was in Year Seven. He didn't let the fear of other people stop him from being himself, and neither should I.

"How was crazy golf?" Dad asks as we walk into the house.

By the time we get back to Grandma's, I'm so tired that all I can think about is going to bed. Turns out Isaiah and I are both terrible at crazy golf. I didn't get any holes-in-one but it doesn't matter. I had a laugh hanging around with my friends, just having fun.

"It was brilliant," Mum says, passing him the pizza we picked up on the way back. "Is everything sorted?"

"What's sorted?" I ask. Isaiah stands next to me with his

arms folded, wondering too.

"What do I always say?" Dad smiles as Isaiah and I stand in confusion. "Williams family night needs every single Williams," he says, opening the kitchen door.

"Minnie!"

Almost knocking me over, Minnie runs towards me and I leap forward, giving her the biggest hug.

"But Minnie being here can only mean one thing," Isaiah says, working it all out.

We're going home.

CHAPTER 27

I pull my duvet over my face as the bright light seeps through my bedroom curtains. The warmth of my bed makes me want to lie here all day, but Minnie's wet nose pressed against my face forces me to sit up. I stroke her belly as she turns on her side with a huge grin on her face. It feels good to be back in my bedroom. I look around and see no leftover pizza. No dirty socks on the floor. No Isaiah hammering on the sewing machine or playing the guitar.

I'm finally home.

I get changed for school and head downstairs. Looking around the kitchen and living room, I now understand why we had to stay with Grandma for so long. It's not just mum's kitchen island that's new. Everything downstairs has been completely redone. The walls, the carpet and even most of the furniture has been replaced. Nothing feels the same. It feels strange, like I'm walking into a new house. But seeing Isaiah causing absolute chaos in the kitchen, Dad singing loudly in the shower and Mum's roller skates taking pride of place on the back doorstep, I realize that the important things haven't changed at all.

I go to the front doorstep, waiting for Isaiah. I open my bag to make sure that I haven't left anything at Grandma's. Even though I absolutely hated sharing a room with Isaiah, I'm going to miss seeing Grandma every day. She's promised to come to family night every week from now on.

I have maths support this morning during form period. After speaking with Mum and Dad, I'm okay with going to the group if it means that I'll get better at maths. I've promised that I will ask for help when I need it – and not just for maths. Joining the athletics club has made me realize that you can run your own race and be part of a team at the same time and, sometimes, the biggest victories are those that we achieve together.

"Hey, Storm, grab this," Isaiah says, chucking me a bin bag full of his fashion-show outfits. I catch the bag and follow him out of the garden gate and across the road as we head to school. See. Even Mr Perfect needs help every once in a while.

* * *

I ask Asha to save me a space at the fashion show when she leaves early for lunch.

"Why are you getting up?" Abdul asks Ryan as he packs away too.

"It's a secret," he smiles.

"Excellent lesson today, Ryan," Ms Morrison smiles. "You're Pupil of the Lesson along with Storm for your fabulous 3D model of the solar system." I'm actually impressed with how good our model turned out to be. It's so good that Ms Morrison has decided to hang it from the ceiling by her desk. It was all Ryan though. I just painted where he told me to. And this is perfect timing, because Ryan has now gone a whole week without getting into trouble. Ms Morrison said that she's going to give him another chance and will take him off the yellow report. I've forgotten how many last chances Ryan has had, but I'm glad he's been given another. When Ms Morrison lets us out, I rush down the main hall to find my seat next to Asha and Koko.

Everyone screams as the lights go down and music starts playing. I turn to the stage and see Ryan. My jaw drops. "Has he gatecrashed?" Koko says.

Ryan starts playing the drums next to Mr Johnson. He continues to play as Mrs Osei walks out and struts down the runway. She does a twirl at the end and everyone cheers.

266

As Mrs Osei walks back, Ms Morrison emerges from behind the curtains. Everyone claps as she bounces down the catwalk. You would never guess that she's wearing our old tent. Next up, Mr Peterson steps out from behind the curtain in a leather jacket that is glowing with lights, sewn on by Isaiah, rainbow-painted jeans and Dad's old army boots. Even Mr Johnson has stopped playing to stare in amazement.

Isaiah comes onto the stage at the end to the biggest round of applause. I have to give it to him. He can be super annoying, but he never disappoints. "Firstly, I want to thank the teachers for taking part. It's not easy to come on stage in front of you lot, especially for something like this. Give it up for the teachers!" Isaiah claps loudly and the crowd joins in, some whooping and cheering.

"And now," Isaiah continues, "we're going to end the show with a special solo performance. Please give it up for Ryan Taylor!"

Ryan stands up from behind the drums and walks slowly to the mic at the front of the stage. Handing him a guitar, Isaiah nods to him and Ryan takes the spotlight. He's hesitating. Looking out into the crowd – I hope he can see me. He does and I mouth, "You can do it."

"Hey Jude," he starts, before the whole hall erupts in cheers. By the time he gets to the chorus, every single person in the hall is singing along. When he sings his final note, everyone is on their feet cheering. I see Mr Johnson cheering on the side, while Ms Morrison and Mrs Osei clap loudly.

"I think Pankhurst House is in safe hands with our latest band member," Isaiah smiles. He takes a bow before leaving the stage with his face full of pride.

"How did you manage that?" Koko asks as Ryan sits down beside us.

"I've been practising with Isaiah. It was Mr Johnson's idea after I told him why I missed my guitar lesson."

I root through my blazer pocket, suddenly remembering the sheet of paper from our music lesson weeks ago. "I kept this, just in case you wanted to do the showcase," I say, passing Ryan the sheet of paper with his music beats written on. He grins and puts it safely in his pocket.

"Cheers, Storm, I wouldn't have performed today if you hadn't told me to explain about the music lesson to Mr Johnson. I probably wouldn't have bothered going again."

"That's what friends are for, right?" I reply, nudging him with my shoulder and smiling.

"Right," he says, smiling back.

"Please welcome Mrs Osei back to the stage for a special announcement." Isaiah claps as Mrs Osei struts back onto the stage. She gives the audience a twirl, not quite ready to end her catwalk.

"Now, it's not every year that I get the joy of announcing victory for Daisy Mill," she begins.

My stomach flutters, as I realize where this is going. "After fifteen long years of trying, we were victorious in becoming the Greater Manchester Schools Athletics Champions!"

The whole crowd whoops loudly. "Could the athletics team please make their way to the stage." I stand up and walk towards the stage. Razan and Edie follow behind as each team-member soaks up the glory.

"Storm, please can you do the honours of presenting the trophy," Mrs Osei says, placing the athletics championship trophy into my hands.

Standing up here with all eyes on me would usually send me into a complete panic, but I keep my head up and take a step forwards, lifting the trophy up in the air to rapturous applause.

When Mr Harris asked me to be on the athletics team, I hesitated. I mean, me? Joining in and standing in the spotlight? It wasn't something that I could ever imagine doing at the beginning of the year. But I've found something that I love to do. I joined a club, won my races and helped Daisy Mill win the championships. I'm going to be the flag-bearer on Sports Day and lead my team out onto the field, something that would've absolutely terrified me a few months ago. I'm always going to find social situations a bit scary, but I'm not going to let that stop me from taking part. From joining in, I've made friends; real friends, who don't want me to hide my interests or change my appearance. I've got better at reading in class without tripping over my words, and I can ask for help when I need it. I can stand up for myself, even to people with louder voices. And I did all of this just by being myself.

Quiet Storm.

ACKNOWLEDGEMENTS

Thank you to Gyamfia Osei for believing in *Quiet Storm* right from the beginning. You championed this story through the messy first drafts and I am forever grateful and blessed to have you in my corner. You really are the best agent ever.

To Rebecca Hill, Alice Moloney and everybody at Usborne. Thank you for giving me the opportunity to give Storm a voice.

Thank you to Bex Glendining for creating the most perfect front cover.

To my family for all the support – Mum, Dad, Schvearn, Katherine, Craig and Teddy. Thank you to my grandparents for passing on your love of reading to me.

Faryal – you were the first person I told about *Quiet Storm*. Thank you for the car rides where we sang (badly), laughed too much and where you listened to all my publishing talk.

To my past students at Whalley Range High School – you're all grown up now but I'll never forget working with such brilliant young girls. My heart will forever be purple.

To my current students at Trinity CofE High School – you are a constant joy and inspiration to be around. Trinity students are the most talented young people out there and no one can tell me differently.

To the 0G6 kitchen crew – thanks for keeping me sane and motivated. Work would not be the same without you guys or our break time chats.

And to my readers, I hope you too are brave enough to live aloud. We all deserve to shine.